Tom tu___ _ rou___ _nd smiled. 'Hello, Amy___ __ me i__o_uce you. Th_ _ P_rdy._

Be polite, smile, but keep your distance, Amy told herself. It isn't your job to fix this. 'Hello, Perdy,' she said, staying exactly where she was.

'Hello, Miss Rivers,' Perdy said dutifully.

That sounded so stuffy and formal. Completely not how Amy was. For a moment she was tempted to offer her own first name; then her common sense kicked in. *Keep your distance.* Formality would help her to do that. She gave the little girl a polite smile.

'I'll, um, let you get on,' Amy said. 'I just wanted to introduce myself—that was all. See you later.' She fled for sanctuary.

Though not before she heard Perdy ask Tom, 'Did she go because of me?' And she could almost see the wobble in the little girl's lower lip, the distress on her face.

'No, honey, of course not. She's just got things to do,' Tom said.

Which made Amy feel even more horrible inside. She'd have to find some middle ground. Surely she could be kind to the little girl without taking down the barrie____ ____ ___

She'd m___

Just n___ _____ ___ ___ ___ _me back t_

Dear Reader

I really enjoy second-chance stories—and in this case Amy, my heroine, needs a second chance at her career as well as at love. When life steamrollers over her, it's natural for her to come home to the place where she was so happy as a child (which just so happens to be on the Norfolk coast—my own favourite place in the world). But when she ends up sharing a house with her uncle's locum, she finds herself having to confront the distant past as well as her recent difficulties.

Tom also needs a second chance at love—with someone who'll love him and be a real mother to his beloved daughter.

Perdy stole my heart (probably because she has much in common with my own beloved daughter at that age—beachcombing and baking are such fun). And getting them all to have a happy ending, as a family, was a real joy.

Add in a gorgeous dog, the history of medicine, a medical specialty that really fascinates me, and a house with a turret (my fantasy house!), and I think you can see why I found NEUROSURGEON...AND MUM! such a pleasure to write.

I'm always delighted to hear from readers, so do come and visit me at www.katehardy.com

With love

Kate Hardy

NEUROSURGEON...
AND MUM!

BY
KATE HARDY

MILLS & BOON

First published in Great Britain 2010
Harlequin Mills & Boon Limited,
Eton House, 18-24 Paradise Road, Richmond, Surrey TW9 1SR

© Pamela Brooks 2010

ISBN: 978 0 263 87904 9

Harlequin Mills & Boon policy is to use papers that are natural, renewable and recyclable products and made from wood grown in sustainable forests. The logging and manufacturing process conform to the legal environmental regulations of the country of origin.

Printed and bound in Spain
by Litografia Rosés, S.A., Barcelona

Kate Hardy lives in Norwich, in the east of England, with her husband, two young children, one bouncy spaniel, and too many books to count! When she's not busy writing romance or researching local history, she helps out at her children's schools. She also loves cooking—spot the recipes sneaked into her books! (They're also on her website, along with extracts and stories behind the books.) Writing for Mills & Boon has been a dream come true for Kate—something she wanted to do ever since she was twelve. She now writes Medical™ romances and also writes for Modern Heat™. She says it's the best of both worlds, because she gets to learn lots of new things when she's researching the background to a book: add a touch of passion, drama and danger, a new gorgeous hero every time, and it's the perfect job!

Kate's always delighted to hear from readers, so do drop in to her website at www.katehardy.com

Recent titles by the same author:

Medical™ Romance
THE DOCTOR'S LOST-AND-FOUND BRIDE
FALLING FOR THE PLAYBOY MILLIONAIRE
 (The Brides of Penhally Bay)

Modern Heat™
GOOD GIRL OR GOLD-DIGGER?
TEMPORARY BOSS, PERMANENT MISTRESS

Praise for
Kate Hardy:

'THE CHILDREN'S DOCTOR'S SPECIAL PRO-POSAL is just as the title promises. Kate Hardy delivers a superb romance that resonates beautifully with the reader. Bravo, Ms Hardy!'

—bookilluminations.com

'THE GREEK DOCTOR'S NEW-YEAR BABY is romantic storytelling at its best! Poignant, enjoyable and absolutely terrific, with THE GREEK DOCTOR'S NEW-YEAR BABY Kate Hardy proves once again that when it comes to romantic fiction she's up there with the very best!'

—cataromance.com

'SURRENDER TO THE PLAYBOY SHEIKH: I spent a lovely morning with this book, and I'd advise you to do likewise. Get it. You'll love it. An unrestrained...Grade: A.'

—goodbadandunread.com

'PLAYBOY BOSS, PREGNANCY OF PASSION: this story features a strong heroine who gains strength from her family and a hero who realises the importance of love and family before it's too late. Add in their captivating romance and it makes for one great read.'

—RT Book Reviews

CHAPTER ONE

TOM finally found Perdy curled up in a chair with a book in the corner of the room; her face was wary, and she was clearly trying to be quiet and keep out of the way. Not for the first time, his heart burned in his chest. It wasn't supposed to be like this. Eloise should have been here beside him, making a proper family: the two of them and their precious daughter. And Perdy should have been a normal child, messy and laughing and seeing rainbows in every corner instead of shadows.

He clenched his jaw for a second, willing the anger to die down. Stop being an idiot, he told himself. You know it's irrational, being angry with Eloise. Just stop blaming her for getting that tropical fever and dying.

But he couldn't.

On my own, he thought, am I making a complete mess of bringing up Perdy? Eloise hadn't exactly been a hands-on mother, but at least he'd been able to talk to her and come to a joint decision; on his own, he had nobody to bounce ideas off, nobody to warn him that he was doing the wrong thing.

He smiled at his daughter, but she didn't smile back. Had he made the wrong decision, bringing her here, away from London? Maybe he should've toughed it out instead of dragging his daughter off in the middle of the school year to make a new start in a place where nobody knew them. But London hadn't really been healthy for Perdy, either. All that pity for the poor motherless child had made Perdy withdraw further and further inside herself.

And he hadn't been able to reach her.

Seeing the ad for a locum GP in a coastal town in Norfolk had seemed like the answer to his problems. Three months. Long enough to give Perdy a chance to settle and give them both the new start they so badly needed. He could rent out their little terraced house for three months; if it worked out in Norfolk, he could find a permanent job there and they could sell up, but if Perdy missed the bustle of the city too much they could still move back. Doing it this way kept all their options open. And Joe and Cassie Rivers had been so warm, so welcoming, even offering him somewhere to stay; the way they'd put it, they needed someone to house-sit while they were in Australia, so he and Perdy would be doing them a favour.

But although they'd been here for almost two weeks now, Perdy was still quiet. She'd been perfectly polite to everyone, but it seemed she'd put up this huge glass wall.

And Tom didn't have anyone to ask to help him break it down.

His own parents were old, growing fragile; he couldn't lean on them. And Eloise's parents...well, they were the reason why his wife had been the way she was, why she'd never been satisfied with her achievements but had always striven to do more. No way was he going to let them do the same thing to his daughter.

'Hey.' He sat on the arm of her chair and ruffled her hair. 'You OK?'

She looked up from her book. 'Yes, Daddy.'

'Good book?'

'Yes, Daddy.'

He tried again. 'What's it about?'

She shrugged. 'A boy who has to dig holes.'

He could've guessed that from the title and the picture on the front cover. Clearly she didn't want to discuss it; she kept glancing back at the page, as if wanting to be polite to her father but desperate to get back to her story.

Hell, hell, hell. He didn't want polite. He wanted her to love him, the way he loved her. He wanted a normal child, one who was noisy and messy and cheeky…and *secure*.

He reached down to hug her, breathing in the scent of her hair. His little girl. She'd been the light of his life for the last eight years. Even now he looked at her and marvelled that she was his. 'OK, honey. I'll let you get back to your reading.' Though he wasn't going to stop trying to get through to her. He'd push just a little, each day. To let her know that he was there, that he'd still be there when she was finally ready to talk. He swallowed hard. 'You do know I love you very, very much, don't you?'

'Yes, Daddy. I love you, too.'

They were the words he wanted to hear but her voice was quiet, colourless, and he didn't quite believe them. The loss of Eloise had broken his little girl's heart, and all the love inside her had seemed to drain away. And he didn't know how to begin to fix things.

Should he try to find her a new mother, maybe?

No. It wouldn't help Perdy and it certainly wouldn't help him. Eloise had broken his heart, too, and he never wanted to get involved with anyone again. Though that wasn't because he thought he'd be in love with his wife for the rest of his days; at times, he *really* hated Eloise. And then he felt guilty for resenting her so much, and the cycle of hurt began all over again.

'Don't read too late. You've got school tomorrow. Jammies, teeth and bed in twenty minutes, OK?'

'Yes, Daddy.'

A nasty thought struck him. Perdy was quiet and booky. A bully's dream. Was she...? 'Is school all right?' Please, God, let her have made friends. Children who could make a better job of protecting her against the world than he had.

She nodded, and Tom had the distinct feeling that, if anything, his little girl was trying to protect him. Maybe he'd call her teacher tomorrow after morning surgery, have a quiet word with her and find out how Perdy had really settled. 'OK, honey. I'll let you get on with your book. And in half an hour I'll come upstairs to tuck you in.'

This time her smile was pure gratitude.

And it broke the pieces of his heart into even smaller fragments.

Amy wrapped her hands round the mug of hot milk, but it wasn't soothing her or making her feel warm. It wasn't keeping the nightmare away.

The same nightmare she'd had for months. Seeing Ben on the operating table in front of her. Trying so hard to fix the nerves in his spine and the crack in his vertebra, trying to keep the emotion blocked off while she worked, trying to stem her growing horror when she realised that she couldn't do it. And Laura's voice in her head, full of pain and betrayal and misery: I trusted you...

The dream always made her wake in a cold sweat.

Worse still, because when she woke she knew it hadn't been a dream.

Every single bit of it had happened.

She shivered, more from misery than cold. Right now she couldn't see a way forward. A way to get rid of the shadows.

Fergus Keating had told her to take three months off.

What on earth was she going to do with herself for three whole months?

Though she knew the head of neurosurgery was right. She wasn't capable of doing her job properly, she was a liability to the team, and she needed to sort her head out. He'd been kind enough to refuse her resignation and suggest a sabbatical instead.

He'd also suggested that she tried going to counselling, but she couldn't see the point. Talking to someone wasn't going to get Ben's mobility back, was it? Or make her best friend forgive her. Her best friend of half a lifetime, who never wanted to see her again. She dragged in a breath. The loss of Laura hurt more than anything else. Now was the time she should've been able to support Laura through a rough patch, listen to her, be there for her. But how could you support someone when you were the one who'd caused all the problems?

Fergus's other suggestion sat more easily with her: to get out of London, away from everything, and give herself enough space to decide what she wanted to do. And Amy knew exactly where she wanted to go.

Not that she was selfish enough to call her favourite aunt at four in the morning.

Somehow, she managed to stumble through the day, promising herself that she wouldn't ring before the evening. That she'd pull herself together before she rang.

And at five to seven she punched the number into her phone with shaking fingers.

Please, please, let her be there.

'Cassie Rivers speaking.'

'Aunt Cassie? It's Amy. I was wondering...can I come down at the weekend and stay for a bit, please?'

Amy's aunt blew out a breath. 'Love, you know you're always welcome here, but I'm afraid Joe and I are off to Australia, the day after tomorrow.'

Of course they were. Her cousin Beth's first baby was due in a month, and Cassie and Joe wanted to go and spend some time with their only daughter and their very first grandchild. Cassie had been bubbling about it for weeks. What kind of selfish, thoughtless person could forget about something like that?

The same kind of person who'd wrecked her best friend's life.

She dragged her thoughts back together. 'Sorry, Cassie. I wasn't thinking.'

But maybe some of the misery in her voice communicated itself to her aunt, because Cassie said gently, 'More like you're too tired to remember. You drive yourself too hard, love.'

And had done so ever since she'd started her neurosurgeon's training. She'd wanted to be among the best in her field. She'd been bang on target, until she'd screwed up so badly with Ben. And since then everything had fallen apart. Not that she'd talked to anyone about it; even if her parents hadn't been thousands of miles away in the States, she couldn't have talked to them about her failure, and she hadn't wanted to lean on her aunt and uncle. In the circumstances, talking to Laura wasn't an option: so she'd just had to suck it up and deal with it by herself.

She'd failed at that, too.

'I'm OK,' she said neutrally.

'Look, love, even though we're not going to be here,

you're welcome to come and spend some time here. How long were you thinking of staying?'

'I'm not sure.'

'A few days? A week?' Cassie suggested.

'I'm, um, taking a sabbatical. Maybe a couple of weeks, if that's OK?'

'A fortnight isn't a sabbatical, it's a break. But you're not on holiday, are you?' Cassie asked perceptively. 'What's happened?'

'I just need a bit of time to think things through,' Amy prevaricated.

'All right, love.'

Amy heard the subtext clearly: *I won't push until you're ready to talk about it.*

Bless her.

'Stay for as long as you like. We'll be back in six weeks, and you're more than welcome to stay after we get back,' Cassie continued. 'You can house-sit for us while we're away. And your being here means we won't have to put Buster in kennels.'

Typical Cassie. Putting it in a way that made Amy feel she wasn't doing all the taking—and in a way that she couldn't refuse. 'Thanks, Cassie. I'd like that. And I'll make sure I take him for a walk every day.' The chocolate Labrador was elderly now, but Amy could still remember her aunt and uncle getting him as a pup, when she'd stayed for the summer holidays before her finals.

'Joe's locum is staying, too, but there's plenty of room—he won't get in your way.'

Joe's locum was the real house-sitter, Amy guessed. So Cassie probably hadn't even booked Buster into kennels in the first place. 'Are you sure you don't mind?'

'Of course we don't, love.' There was a pause. 'Amy,

why don't you throw your stuff in a bag, get in the car and come down right now? It sounds as if you could do with a good meal and a chat.'

Amy almost cracked. Unconditional love and support was something she wanted so badly—but something she knew she really didn't deserve. Not after what she'd done. Besides, Joe and Cassie were so excited about Australia and the new baby. She couldn't bring herself to worry them with her own problems when they were about to go to the other side of the world. 'Thanks, but I have a few things I need to sort out in London.'

'All right, then we'll talk now.'

Panic made Amy catch her breath. 'You must be in the middle of packing. Don't let me hold you up, Cassie. Honestly, I'm fine. I just need a bit of time off. You know how you're always nagging me about working too hard.'

Cassie didn't sound so sure about it, but to Amy's relief she didn't push it. 'Well, we'll leave the key in the usual place. And I'll text you when we get to Australia. You know you can me call any time—though remember we're nine hours ahead of you, in Melbourne.'

'I will. And thanks, Cassie.' For the bolthole. For the breathing space. For not pushing her.

'Any time, love.'

'Give my love to Beth. I hope she gets an easy de-livery—and I want to see a picture of the baby as soon as you're allowed to take one, OK?'

'You can count on it, love,' Cassie said. 'Drive safely.'

'I will,' Amy promised. 'Have a good trip.'

CHAPTER TWO

On Thursday morning, just as the rush hour ended, Amy left London for Norfolk. By lunchtime, she'd reached the large seaside town where her uncle had lived ever since Amy was tiny. The place where she'd spent many happy summers. The place that might just help her to sort her head out.

She parked on the gravelled area in front of Marsh End House; there was no other car there, so she assumed that the locum was on duty at the surgery, unless maybe he didn't have a car. She went to the fifth large cobble stone in the flower border to the right of the front door and lifted it; as she expected, the front door key sat underneath it. She let herself in and heard a volley of excited barks from the kitchen; as soon as she opened the door, Buster nearly knocked her flying.

She knelt down on the floor and made a fuss of him. 'You're meant to be a staid old dog, not a bouncy pup,' she admonished him with a smile. 'Look at all the grey in your face. And you're still just like you were twelve years ago.'

Buster responded by resting his front paws on her shoulders and licking her face enthusiastically.

'You big old softie,' she said. 'OK, let me bring my stuff in and have a cup of tea and then I'll take you for a run.'

His tail thumped madly, and she grinned. 'It's so good to be home.' Funny, Cassie and Joe's place had always been home to her—more so than her parents' house in London or her own flat, even. Marsh End House was a Victorian Gothic masterpiece, built of red brick with arched windows, lots of pointed gables and an elaborate turret that had been the centre of the games she'd played with Beth and her two younger brothers in those long, hot summers. Games of wizards and princesses and magic castle—followed by sandcastle competitions on the beach, games of cricket and football and exploring the rockpools at low tide. Here was where she'd always been happiest.

And best of all was the kitchen, right in the heart of the house. Where scraped knees had been washed, kissed better and covered with a dressing; the cake tin had always been full; and, as they had grown older, the kettle had always been hot and Cassie always there to listen and not judge.

So many wonderful memories.

Would they be enough to heal her now?

There was an envelope with her name on it propped against the biscuit tin in the middle of the kitchen table. Recognising her aunt's handwriting, Amy opened it.

Have made a bed for you in your old room.

In the turret. Fabulous. She'd be overlooking the marshes towards the sea, her favourite view in the world, and the sun would wake her every morning. And maybe here she wouldn't have the nightmares.

Tom will introduce himself and Perdy to you at some point.

So the locum was married? Well, that wasn't a problem; the house was big enough for them not to get in each other's way.

Make sure you eat properly.

She couldn't help smiling. The first thing Cassie did to everyone was to feed them. Though Amy knew her aunt had a point; she hadn't been able to summon up the energy to make a proper meal for months. She'd been living on sandwiches and canteen food, and picking even at those. Maybe the sea air would help to bring back her appetite.

There was a postscript in Joe's atrocious handwriting: if she found herself at a loose end, there was a box in his study with some of Joseph Rivers's casebooks. She might want to take a look through them and put them in some sort of order. There were more in a box in the attic, if she wanted to bring them down.

Joseph had been the first surgeon in the family, back in the late 1820s; for years both Joe and her father had talked of sorting out his papers and doing something with the casebooks. But her father had been offered a professorship in cardiac surgery in the States and Joe had been busy with his GP practice, so it had never happened. Once or twice Carrie had suggested that maybe the next generation would like to do it but, the last time the subject had been raised, Beth had been busy carving out a career in computing, Joey and Martin had been studying for their finals and Amy had just switched specialties to neurosurgery, which had absorbed every second of her time. And so nothing had ever happened with Joseph's papers.

Maybe looking through his papers might help her remember why she'd become a doctor in the first place, Amy thought. Or give her a clue as to where her path led now. Because, right now, she had no idea what was going to happen with the rest of her life. It was like staring into a tunnel without even a pinprick of light at the end. Even thinking about it made her feel as if she were suffocating in blackness. And she felt so very, very alone.

She lugged her suitcase upstairs to her room and left it at the end of the bed before heading back to the kitchen to put the kettle on. She was halfway through a cup of tea, a sandwich and the cryptic crossword in the newspaper she'd bought on impulse that morning when the front door opened.

Buster gave a sharp bark to warn her that someone was there, and then a warmer, more welcoming woof, and skidded up the hallway to greet the person who'd just walked in.

'Hey, Buster. Go find your Frisbee and we'll have ten minutes in the garden.'

This must be Tom, the locum, Amy thought. He had a nice voice, deep and calm with the slightest trace of a London accent.

Just as she registered it, he walked into the kitchen. 'Hello. You must be Amy. I'm Tom Ashby.'

He was in his early thirties, she'd guess, around her own age; he had a shock of dark wavy hair that he'd brushed back from his forehead, very fair skin, and hazel eyes hidden behind wire-framed glasses. His smile was polite enough, but there was a seriousness to him and an intensity that made her wonder what he'd look like if he let himself relax and laughed. Whether his mouth would soften into a sexy grin and his eyes would crinkle at the corners.

Not that it was any of her business. She already knew that Tom was unavailable; in any case, relationships weren't her thing. Since the wreckage of her engagement to Colin, ten years before, she'd kept all dates light and very, very casual; she was just fine and dandy on her own.

'Hello.' Amy shook Tom's proffered hand. 'Cassie left me a note. She said you'd introduce yourself and Perdy at some point.'

'Perdy's at school.'

So Tom's wife was a teacher. 'I see,' Amy said, giving

him a polite smile and hoping that by the time Perdy came home she'd have managed to find a stock of small talk.

Amy Rivers was nothing like Tom had imagined. For a start, she was gorgeous. Too thin, and there was a pallor in her face to go with the bagginess in her clothes that told him she hadn't been looking after herself properly, but she was still beautiful. Her sea-green eyes reminded him of Joe's; her dark hair was cut very short and yet managed to be feminine rather than making her look aggressive or butch. Her mouth was a perfect rosebud; it made him want to reach out and trace her lower lip with the tip of his finger.

Not that he was going to give in to the impulse.

Apart from the fact that Amy Rivers could already be involved with someone and wouldn't welcome his advances, there was Perdy to consider. She'd had enough upheaval in her life, and the last year had been seriously rough. She really didn't need her father forgetting himself and behaving like a teenager. So Tom knew he had to treat Amy just as if she were another colleague, even though they didn't actually work together. Polite enough to avoid any friction, but distant enough not to get involved. Keep everything to small talk.

'How was your journey?' he asked politely.

'Fine, thanks. I got stuck behind a tractor three miles out of town, but that's par for the course around here at this time of year.' She indicated her mug. 'The kettle's hot. Can I get you a coffee or something?'

'That'd be nice. Thanks.'

'How do you like it?'

'Just milk, no sugar, please.'

She switched the kettle on and shook instant coffee into a mug. 'So Buster's suckered you into playing Frisbee with him. Have you taught him to drop it yet?'

'I wish. He normally leaves it under the trees at the bottom of the garden and waits for me to fetch it.'

'You'd never believe his pedigree's full of field trial champions, would you?' Amy finished making the coffee and handed the mug to Tom.

His fingers brushed against hers and desire zinged down his spine.

Not good. It was the first time he'd felt that pull of attraction since Eloise. Given how badly that had ended, he wasn't prepared to take a second risk—even if Amy Rivers turned out to be single.

'Cassie says you're staying for a while,' he said, deliberately putting the whole length of the table between them. Not that it stopped him noticing her face was heart shaped. Or how fine her fingers were, wrapped around her mug of tea. No ring on her left hand: not that that meant anything nowadays. You didn't have to be married to be committed. But she had beautiful hands. Delicate hands. An artist's hands, maybe? Neither Cassie nor Joe had told him much about Amy. Just that she was their niece, she lived in London, and she was taking some time out from her job. Cassie had looked worried, which implied that there was a problem with Amy's job, but Tom hadn't pressed for details; it wasn't his place to ask.

'Don't worry, I won't get in your way,' she said, her face shuttering.

And now he'd put her back up. 'I'm sorry, I didn't intend to suggest that you would. There's plenty of room for all of us. I was just thinking, maybe we could all eat together. It seems a bit pointless, cooking separately. But that doesn't mean I expect you to do all the cooking,' he added hastily. 'Maybe we can share the chores.'

'Sure.' She still looked slightly wary: a look he'd seen

all too often on his daughter's face. Meaning that she wanted space.

'Look, I'll go and wear Buster out a bit, then I've got a couple of house calls to make,' he said.

'You're not stopping for lunch?'

'I'll get something later.'

She bit her lip. 'Look, I meant it about not getting in your way. And don't feel you're obliged to entertain me or anything.'

'Ditto,' he said. 'As far as I'm concerned, we're sharing the house and looking after the dog for Joe and Cassie. And we're sharing chores because it makes sense. It's more efficient.'

She was silent for a moment, and then she nodded. 'Agreed. Well, I ought to stop lazing around and unpack. I'll catch you later.'

'What about your sandwich?' he asked. She'd eaten less than half of it, he noticed.

'Did Cassie ask you to watch my eating?' Amy asked.

He felt himself flush. 'No. Just that I didn't want you to feel I was pushing you out of the kitchen before you'd finished.' Was that what the problem was? Amy had some kind of eating disorder and it had caused her to have a breakdown at work? In which case she must have interpreted his suggestion of eating together as pushing her, too. This was going to be a minefield.

To his surprise, she smiled. 'Thank you. And, no, I don't have any kind of eating disorder.'

He groaned. 'Did I say that out loud? I apologise.'

'No, you just have an expressive face,' Amy said dryly. 'I admit, I haven't been eating properly lately, because I've been busy at work and when you're under pressure and rushed for time it's easier to grab fast food. That, or wait until you get home and it's so late that you're too tired to bother with more than a bit of toast. But you don't have to worry that you'll starve when it's my turn to make dinner. Cassie taught me to cook.'

Why hadn't Amy's mother taught her? Tom wondered.

Or maybe Amy's mother was the kind of mother that his wife had been. Distant. Feeling trapped. Wanting to do her own thing and wishing that she'd never got married and had a child to hold her back.

'Sorry. I shouldn't be prying,' he said. And he certainly didn't want to answer any questions about his own past. 'How about I cook for us tonight?'

'You've been at work.'

He shrugged. 'And you've had a long drive, which I'd say is more tiring—especially as I know there are road-works on the motorway and you've probably been stuck in traffic for a while. It's no problem. Really.'

'Then I'll wash up,' she said.

'Deal.' Though he didn't offer to shake on it. Because he had a feeling that once he touched Amy Rivers, he'd want more. A lot more. And it would get way, way too complicated.

She'd vanished by the time he'd finished playing with Buster. He made himself a sandwich, checked the dog's water bowl was full then headed out on his house calls.

'I hear young Amy's back,' Mrs Poole, his first patient, said as he removed the dressing to check the ulcer just above her ankle.

He looked up at her, surprised. 'Wow. The grapevine's fast around here.' Amy couldn't have arrived more than a couple of hours ago.

'Well, a car with a registration plate saying "AMY" parked outside Marsh End House has to be hers, doesn't it?' She shrugged. 'Not that she's been down here for a while now. Funny that she decides to turn up this week, with Joe and Cassie just off to Australia.'

Tom didn't appreciate gossip about himself and he had a feeling that Amy would be the same. 'She's house- and dog-sitting for her aunt and uncle.'

'I thought that was what you were supposed to be doing.'

'You know what they say. Many hands make light work,' Tom said with a smile, and concentrated on checking the ulcer for granulation.

'Used to spend every summer here, she did. Too quiet by miles for the first week, but by the end of the summer she was getting as grubby as the boys and plotting all kinds of things with young Beth.'

Too quiet. Just as his own daughter was. But Amy had had her cousins to help her out of her shell. Perdy had nobody except him, and so far he was a big fat failure.

He changed the subject swiftly. 'I'm really pleased with the way you're healing. So you've been keeping your leg up, as I suggested?'

'Yes. Though I hate sitting still.' Mrs Poole tutted. 'I've never been one to sit and do nothing.'

'Gentle exercise is fine,' Tom said. 'But if you overdo it, the ulcer will take longer to heal. You don't have to sit around all the time, just make sure you rest with your leg up for half an hour, three or four times a day, to take the pressure off your veins.' He cleaned the ulcer gently then put a fresh dressing on, topping it with an elastic bandage. 'Can you circle your ankle for me, Mrs Poole, so I can check that bandage isn't too tight for you?'

She did so, and he smiled. 'That's fine. I'll come and see you tomorrow afternoon. In the meantime, if it starts to hurt more or your foot feels hotter or colder, or you notice it's changed colour, ring the surgery straight away—please don't wait.' In his experience, elderly people fell into two camps: the ones who were lonely, desperately wanted company and would ring up if they so much as cut their finger; and those who didn't want to make a fuss and would leave it until their condition had really deteriorated before they admitted that they needed help. Mrs Poole was definitely one of the latter, or her ulcer wouldn't have spread so badly.

'I'll be fine, Doctor,' she said. 'You don't need to worry about me.'

He rather thought he did. 'I want a promise from you,' he said, giving her his most charming smile, 'or I'll have to go and chat to your neighbours and ask them to set up a roster to check on you every couple of hours between now and my next visit.'

'You can't bother them with that!' She looked aghast.

'Promise me, then.' He squeezed her hand gently. 'I appreciate you want to be independent, which is great, but there is such a thing as being too independent. If you catch a medical condition in the early stages, it's usually easier and quicker to treat it—and it won't hurt you as much.'

'I'm not like that Betty Jacklin—straight on the phone to the surgery, convinced she's got a brain tumour, every time she has a headache.' Mrs Poole rolled her eyes.

Tom hid a smile. He'd already been warned about Betty Jacklin, but hadn't come across her yet. 'I can't possibly comment on other patients. I know you wouldn't call me for something little. But I also know you're the sort who's too stubborn to ring when she really ought to.' He squeezed her hand gently again. 'And guess which kind of patient I lose more sleep over?'

Mrs Poole sighed. 'All right. I promise I'll call you.'

'Thank you.' He smiled at her. 'Do you want me to make you a cup of tea before I go?'

She shook her head. 'You don't have time for that, Doctor.'

He glanced at his watch. 'Actually, I do.' It would only take a couple of minutes. And if it meant getting her to drink a bit more, he was all for it. Too many of his elderly patients didn't drink enough and ended up with bladder infections—which, if not treated fast enough, led to fever and confusion and being cared for in hospital until the antibiotics did their job, not to mention a huge worry for their families. He believed in pre-empting things where he could. 'So, if I remember rightly, that's a dash of milk and half a teaspoon of sugar?'

'You're a good lad, Dr Ashby,' Mrs Poole said. 'And, with your looks, you must have the women lining up for you.'

Tom just smiled. He hadn't noticed any line of women—and even if there was one, he wasn't interested. His daughter came first. And he'd never put himself in the position where his heart could be broken again.

At half past three, Amy was sitting at Joe's desk, starting to look through the box of Joseph's papers, when Buster left his position at her feet and bounded through the door, tail wagging.

Clearly Tom was home.

She could hear a child talking. Odd: Tom hadn't mentioned anything about a child. Unless maybe his wife was doing some extra tuition and one of her pupils had come back with her?

Better get the introductions over with, she thought, and headed out of the office. She followed the sound of voices to the kitchen, noting the child's rucksack hanging up in the hallway. And she blinked in surprise when she walked into the kitchen. There was a little girl sitting at the table—around eight years old, Amy judged—with a glass of milk and a book in front of her. She had Tom's colouring and that same shy, slightly hesitant smile.

Buster pattered across the tiles to her, alerting Tom to the fact that he and the little girl were no longer alone. He turned round and smiled at Amy. 'Hello, Amy. Let me introduce you. This is Perdita—everyone calls her Perdy.'

Perdy was clearly Tom's daughter, then, not his wife.

Carrie hadn't mentioned anyone else. So where was the child's mother? Was Tom divorced? But Amy knew it wasn't that common for fathers to be given custody of the children, which meant that the break-up must've been messy with a capital M.

No wonder Perdy looked quiet and withdrawn.

Amy remembered another little girl being like that, too. A little girl whose father had been awarded custody. A little girl she'd grown to love so much, as if Millie were her own daughter rather than her intended stepchild-to-be.

But then Colin had suggested that they move to the States, to let Millie see more of her mother. And while Amy had been tying up loose ends in England, thinking that she was going to start a new life with the man and child she loved, Colin had changed his mind. He'd called Amy with the news that he and his ex had decided to give their marriage another go, for their daughter's sake. That had been hard enough to take; but then he'd added that he thought that a clean break would be the best thing for Millie.

Amy knew it had been the right thing to do, for the little girl's sake. But it had ripped her world apart, and she'd retreated into work afterwards, concentrating on her career rather than her private life.

Which had worked just fine—until her career had gone so badly wrong, too.

OK, so this wasn't quite the same. She wasn't in any

kind of relationship with Tom Ashby. But, right now, she was bone tired and she just didn't have the strength to help anyone else.

Be polite, smile, but keep your distance, Amy told herself. It isn't your job to fix this. 'Hello, Perdy,' she said, staying exactly where she was.

'Perdy, this is Miss Rivers.'

Miss rather than Doctor. Did he know that she was a qualified surgeon? Or hadn't Joe and Carrie told him that she was a medic of any kind? Not that it made much difference. She wasn't a neurosurgeon any more.

'Hello, Miss Rivers,' Perdy said dutifully.

That sounded so stuffy and formal. Completely not how Amy was. For a moment, she was tempted to offer her own first name; then her common sense kicked in. *Keep your distance.* Formality would help her to do that. She gave the little girl a polite smile. 'Hello.'

'Joe and Carrie are Miss Rivers's aunt and uncle. She's staying here for a while,' Tom explained.

Perdy looked worried for a moment, and then carefully made her face blank. 'Does that mean we have to go and find somewhere else to live?'

It sounded as though they'd moved around a bit, and Amy could remember being much happier here as a child because she was settled for the summer instead of dragging round after her parents with nobody to play with. Guilt flooded through her. What was the old saying? What goes around comes around. Joe and Cassie had been kind to her. She really ought to offer the same kindness to Perdy. It wasn't the little girl's fault that her presence brought back memories of Millie and a sense of loss that Amy would prefer to suppress.

'No, darling, it just means we're sharing the house,' Tom said, ruffling her hair.

'So I can still play with Buster?' Perdy asked.

'Absolutely,' Tom reassured her.

Amy should've guessed that Perdy would respond to the dog in the same way that Amy herself had responded to Joe and Cassie's dogs as a child. Guilt twisted in her stomach again. But this wasn't her problem and she had enough to deal with. She had nothing to offer a lonely little girl. Right now, she had nothing to offer anyone.

'Are you here on a summer holiday, Miss Rivers?' Perdy asked.

'Sort of.'

'Perdy, you're asking too many questions,' Tom said quietly.

The little girl flushed, and shut up.

Amy raised her eyebrows at Tom. OK, so she didn't particularly want to talk about why she was here, but he could have just distracted his daughter instead of putting her down like that.

He looked right back at her, and Amy found herself flushing as deeply as Perdy when she read the message in his eyes. Just who did Amy Rivers think she was, to judge him?

He had a point. She hadn't exactly helped matters, had she? And he was clearly trying to do his best with his little girl.

'I'll, um, let you get on,' Amy said. 'I just wanted to introduce myself, that was all. See you later.' She fled for the sanctuary of Joe's office.

Though not before she heard Perdy ask Tom, 'Did she go because of me?' And she could almost see the wobble in the little girl's lower lip, the distress on her face.

'No, honey, of course not. She's just got things to do,' Tom said.

Which made Amy feel even more horrible inside. She'd

have to find some middle ground. Surely she could be kind to the little girl, without taking down the barriers round her heart?

She'd make the effort, later.

Just not right now, when all the memories had come back to shred her heart all over again.

CHAPTER THREE

THAT evening, after Tom had settled Perdy in bed, he walked into the living room and saw Amy curled up in a chair, reading a book. In Perdy's favourite chair, Tom noticed, the one with a view through the French doors into the garden. Amy was completely engrossed in the words, just like Perdy always was when she had her nose in a book.

And he was intruding.

'Sorry, I didn't realise you were here,' he said, and began to back away.

She looked up. 'It's not a problem. If you want to watch the television or something, that's fine. You won't disturb me.'

'No. But my daughter clearly does.' The words were out before he could stop them, and he kicked himself mentally as colour shot into her face. Couldn't he have found a more tactful way to broach the subject?

'I'm sorry I was a bit abrupt with her,' Amy muttered.

Tom knew he should accept the apology and leave it. But, now he'd started, he couldn't stop himself. Amy hadn't even had dinner with them that evening—she'd made an excuse and shut herself away in the study. And for some reason Perdy had got it into her head that it was because Amy didn't like her—that she was in the way.

'She's eight years old. And it's not as if she's a spoiled brat or running wild.'

'I can see that.'

'So what is it? You don't like kids?'

'It's not that.'

But she didn't look him in the eye; it was obvious that there was something she wasn't telling him. Well, that was her choice. She was an adult, able to make her own decisions; and his main concern was his daughter. 'Look, I don't know how long you plan to be here, and I'll try to keep Perdy out of your way as much as I can, but I'd appreciate it if you could try to be pleasant to her when your paths cross.'

'I'm sorry.' Amy's breath shuddered, as if she was suppressing a sob, and the distress on her face was obvious.

Ah, hell. He'd blundered straight in and made this whole situation worse. Tom raked a hand through his hair. He had to face it, he was hopeless with women. He'd let his wife down, he'd let his daughter down, and now he'd managed to upset the woman he had to share the house with for the next however long. Time to compromise and make the best of this mess. 'So am I. We're guests here in your family's home, and I shouldn't be having a go at you.'

'I'm a guest here, too,' Amy said. 'And you were standing up for your daughter. It's a parent's natural reaction.'

He could see the pain in her eyes before she masked it. So was Amy a parent? And, if so, why wasn't her child with her now?

It was none of his business. He wasn't going to pry. But he had to say something. Give her an explanation for the way he'd snapped at her, at least. 'I'm probably being over-protective. It hasn't been a good year.'

'Yeah. This year's been…' She blew out a breath.

It sounded as if she'd been through the wringer as much as he and Perdy had lately. So maybe they had something in common after all. He sat down. 'That's why we came here. This job seemed like the perfect opportunity—somewhere to make a new start.'

His admission made her expression soften slightly. 'It's a good place,' she said. 'I used to spend my summers here.'

'Holiday home?' he guessed.

'Sort of.' She grimaced. 'My parents were always away on lecturing tours, so it meant either being stuck in London with a nanny, or spending the holidays here with Joe and Cassie.' She smiled, clearly remembering something happy. 'I loved it here. The house was always full of laughter, and I didn't have to be quiet in case I disturbed anyone. I had Cassie and Joe and Beth and the boys, I could share their dog—and, best of all, I knew I was here because they wanted me here, not because they were paid to look after me.'

Amy's childhood sounded very similar to Eloise's, with ambitious parents who didn't pay her enough attention. So had she been damaged the same way as Eloise, Tom wondered, making her desperate to save the world to gain her parents' approval? 'That's why I became a GP rather than working in a hospital—the hours are more regular, and in the days before the practice started using the after-hours service Eloise and I could usually muddle through school holidays between us and not need to use too much child care.'

'Eloise being Perdy's mother, I take it?'

Tom felt the muscle tensing in his jaw. 'Yes.' Now he'd opened up this far, no doubt Amy would ask questions. If he told her the rest, she'd start pitying him. And he'd had enough pity to last a lifetime.

To his surprise, Amy uncurled from her chair. 'I think,' she said, 'we need to agree a truce. And some boundaries.'

'A truce.' That wasn't half of what he was tempted to do with this woman. But he had a feeling that both of them were too mixed up to cope with any kind of relationship right now—not to mention the fact that Amy might be involved with someone.

'I won't ask you about whatever's messed up your past,' she said, 'if you don't ask me about mine.'

'Agreed.' He paused. 'And Perdy?'

She curled up again and wrapped her arms round her legs, resting her chin on her knees. 'I'll try not to be so abrupt.'

'Thank you.' He couldn't ask any more than that. 'So do you know how long you're staying?'

She shrugged. 'My plans are flexible. You?'

'Until a week or so after your uncle and aunt get back from Australia.'

'And you've settled in OK?'

He knew she was being polite rather than really wanting to know. 'Fine.' He had, at least; he wasn't so sure about his daughter. Not that he could discuss that with Amy. She'd made her views on children pretty clear. 'I like it here. Though the village grapevine is pretty effective,' he said ruefully.

'Grapevine?'

'When I saw Mrs Poole on a house call this afternoon, she knew you were back. Though I didn't feed her any gossip. I told her you were dog-sitting.'

The corners of Amy's mouth quirked. 'Tomorrow, you can expect to hear that you're having a hot affair with the wild child from London. So if you have someone in your life who's going to be bothered by that—except your daughter, who already knows we're not involved—you'd better warn her now.'

'There's nobody.' Tom hadn't intended to say that much.

But the picture she'd just put in his head... Oh, lord, he could just imagine it. A hot affair with Amy Rivers. Her mouth softening under his. Her hands in his hair. Finding out how warm and soft her skin was.

He just hoped none of that showed in his expression, or she'd run a mile. 'So were you really a wild child?' he asked.

She gave a short, humourless laugh. 'Far from it. But since when did truth get in the way of a good story?'

'I'm sorry if sharing the house with me is going to make life difficult for you.'

'It won't.' She shrugged. 'If anyone says anything to you, just laugh and ask them if they know where you can get a few more hours in a day, because with a little girl to look after you really don't have time for a love life.'

'That,' Tom said, 'is absolutely true.' And he'd do well to remember that. Any fantasies he might entertain about Amy Rivers had to stay exactly that: fantasies.

On Friday afternoon, Tom was in surgery seeing his last patient before he had to pick up Perdy from the after-school club. Max Barton had passed out at work, and when his colleagues had brought him in Max had said that he felt tired all the time and had to get up at night more frequently to go for a wee. He'd put it down to getting older and putting in more hours at work, but the symptoms—together with Max's ample girth—made Tom suspect something else. He'd also noticed a plaster on Max's thumb, and Max had eventually admitted that he'd cut his hand several days before but the cut just wasn't healing properly. Tom had checked his blood pressure and sent off blood samples, and now the results were back.

'Let's start with the good news, Mr Barton,' he said. 'It's not cancer or heart disease.'

'But?' Max asked.

'Your blood tests,' Tom said gently, 'show that you have type two diabetes. That's the late-onset type, so we can keep it under control with diet and tablets. The good news there is that you're not going to have to inject yourself with insulin.'

Max blew out a breath and relaxed back against the chair. 'I'm so glad. Dad died from a heart attack and I was scared stupid that it might happen to me and the kids would have to grow up without me.'

Yeah. Tom knew all about that feeling. Especially now there was only him; and he resented the fact that Eloise hadn't seemed even to give it a thought before she'd left. Of course saving other people's children was a good thing to do, but did it have to be at the cost of your own?

He snapped his attention back. Not now. His patients had to come first. 'You can put your mind at rest there,' he said gently, 'though I'm afraid there will be a few needles for a bit—you'll need to keep testing your blood sugar levels so we can fine-tune the tablets to suit you. And there are also some things we need to keep an eye on, complications that sometimes come with diabetes, so I'll book you in for the clinic here once a month. Can you remember the last time you had your eyes tested?'

Max spread his hands. 'I've never had a problem with my eyes.'

'Sure,' Tom said, 'but you need to book yourself in and have eye tests at least once a year now, because diabetes can sometimes cause problems with eyes.'

Max frowned. 'So why have I got it? Why me, why now?'

'We don't know why some people get it and not others,' Tom said honestly. 'It's known as late onset because it tends to happen in your forties. Sometimes it runs in families, but not necessarily. Men are twice as likely as women to get it, and you're also more likely to get it if you're overweight and don't do enough exercise.'

'I've always been big,' Max said. 'Everyone in my family's big-boned. But I've cut down on the beer and I always have fruit when someone brings cakes in to work.' He sighed. 'I know I ought to go to the gym or something, but there's never enough time, and to be honest I don't really fancy all that bodybuilding stuff.'

'The fitter you keep yourself,' Tom said, 'and the better you control your diabetes, the less likely you are to develop complications. You don't have to go to the gym. Find something you enjoy doing with your family—that way you'll all get the benefit, whether it's going for a walk or a swim or just kicking a ball around in the park.'

'I suppose we could do that,' Max said.

Tom ran through what the condition involved, how to take the tablets he was about to prescribe and how Max could take readings of his blood sugar and what they meant he needed to do next. 'I'm also going give you some leaflets to take home, including how to get in touch with the local diabetes support group,' Tom said, 'and I'll arrange an appointment for you at the diabetic clinic here at the practice. You're bound to have questions, and we can answer them all there—and your wife's very welcome to come along too. I'll get in touch with the dietician, too. It's a good idea to keep a diary for a week of what you eat, how much and when, and take it along with you to the appointment—it'll save you some time in working things out.'

'So do I have to eat special diabetic foods?'

'Absolutely not.' Tom fished out one of the leaflets and handed it to him. 'It's all about eating healthily. Regular meals, plenty of fruit and veg and foods with a low GI—that means your body absorbs them more slowly and your blood sugar doesn't suddenly spike—and cutting down on salt, sugar and fats. You don't have to eat anything special, and everyone in the family can eat the same as you—it'll be good for them, too.' He smiled at the older man. 'It's a lot to take in all at once, which is one of the reasons why we have leaflets—they'll answer the questions you wish you'd thought of when you're halfway home. But if you're worried about anything at all, just give us a call.' He tapped into the practice system and booked an appointment. 'And Jenny, the practice nurse, will see you on Tuesday morning at ten.'

'Do I have to tell my boss?' Max looked stricken. 'I might lose my job.'

'It's not compulsory, no. But it's a good idea to tell your boss and your colleagues, so they know what to do to help you if you suddenly have a hypo.' Tom explained what would happen if Max's blood sugar suddenly dropped and how people could deal with it. 'You will need to tell the DVLC and your insurance company. But as long as your diabetes is well controlled, it shouldn't be a problem.'

Max closed his eyes and blew out a breath. 'It's a lot to take in. But it's such a relief to know I'm not going to just drop down dead like my dad did.'

Yeah. That was Tom's own biggest fear. If anything happened to him, what would happen to his daughter? He and Eloise had both been only children. There wasn't a family network who could take over. His parents were too old, and Eloise's were as uninterested in their granddaughter as they'd been in their daughter. The only thing they were interested in was her end-of-year school report; and for Tom that was only part of who his daughter was. No way was he going to let them pressure her, the way they'd pressured Eloise.

He pushed the fear aside and concentrated on answering Max's remaining questions, then glanced at his watch. He was going to be late picking Perdy up from after-school club. But he couldn't have rushed his patient out of the door. Sometimes, he thought, juggling single fatherhood with his job was too tricky. And he still hadn't thought about how he was going to cope with the long summer holidays.

Joseph's papers. They were here somewhere, Amy thought, opening a fourth box.

And then she blinked. It was full of books. A quick glance at some of the covers told her they were the ones she and Beth had devoured when they'd been around Perdy's age. Given that Perdy had been reading at the kitchen table yesterday, maybe this would be a good way of apologising for being abrupt. A gesture. Some were probably too old-fashioned now, but she was pretty sure that Perdy would enjoy some of the others. She picked out an armful of the ones she'd enjoyed most, and left them stacked on top of the box while she searched for the box containing Joseph's papers. Once she'd located it and had taken the papers she needed downstairs, she returned to the loft to collect the books. Then, just as she reached the bottom of the stairs, Tom walked through the front door with his daughter.

He brushed a hand against her face and Amy nearly dropped the books as desire shimmered through her. Oh, this was ridiculous. She knew he was single and not involved with anyone, because he'd told her so the previous night; but that didn't mean he was interested in getting involved with her. Whatever had happened between him and Perdy's mother had clearly made him as wary, as Perdy was; and of course there was Perdy to think of.

Not to mention the fact that Amy didn't make the same mistake twice. She'd learned the hard way, through Colin and Millie, that getting involved with a single father was a seriously bad idea. There were way too many complications; and it meant that more than one person ended up with their heart broken when it all ended.

She frowned at Tom, and he said, 'Cobweb.'

Oh. So that was why he'd touched her face. And it wasn't really surprising that she was covered in cobwebs, considering how she'd spent her afternoon. 'I've been rummaging around in the attic,' she explained.

And now for the biggie. Perdy's eyes were averted and she looked uncomfortable. Hardly surprising, given how unwelcoming Amy had been, the previous day.

She took a deep breath. 'Perdy, when I was your age, I used to read a lot, too. And while I was in the attic, I discovered that my aunt kept the books that my cousin Beth and I liked best. So, um, if you'd like to borrow any of them, feel free. I'll leave them stacked on the bookcase, shall I?'

'Thank you, Miss Rivers,' Perdy said politely, though Amy noticed that the little girl still didn't make any kind of eye contact and her face was etched with worry.

First-name terms didn't mean getting involved, did it? Amy swallowed the lump in her throat. 'As we're going to be sharing the house and Buster for a while, until I go back to London, perhaps it'd be easier if you called me Amy.'

She saw the little girl look at her father for guidance, and Tom's brief nod, and her heart ached. How much this reminded her of the time when she'd met Millie. Colin's daughter had been four years old, sweet and shy. Her eyes had been the same serious grey as her father's, and when she'd smiled Amy had discovered that Millie had the same charming dimples as Colin, too. At first Amy had been

'Daddy's friend Amy'. And then she'd earned smiles and hugs in her own right. The night that Millie had asked Amy to read her bedtime story instead of Colin was the moment Amy had realised how much she loved father and daughter, how deeply she'd wanted to be a proper family with them...

'Thank you, Mi—Amy,' Perdy corrected herself, breaking Amy's train of thought and bringing her back to the present.

The expression of pleasure on the little girl's face told Amy that she'd done the right thing. She wasn't getting involved—this time, her heart was definitely going to stay unbroken—but she was making life just that little bit easier for someone else who'd had a rough time.

'What are those?' Tom asked, gesturing to the pile of notebooks on the table in the hallway.

'Joseph's casebooks. He was my...' Amy counted on her fingers '...great-great-great-great-grandfather. The first doctor in the family. He trained in London, but he married a girl from Norwich and moved there.' She smiled. 'Joe's named after him. Actually, it's a family tradition that the eldest son of the eldest son is called Joseph.'

'Why are you looking at his papers?' Perdy asked.

'Uncle Joe asked me if I'd take a look through them while I'm here. He and Dad always meant to sort it out, but as they're both doctors—another family tradition—they were really busy at work and never got round to it.'

'Are you a doctor, too?' Perdy asked.

'I was,' Amy said.

'Does that mean you aren't a doctor now?'

'Perdy,' Tom said quietly, 'shall we go and get you a glass of milk, and a treat for Buster?'

Distraction technique: Amy remembered that one. Although she appreciated it, at the same time she knew that this was something she needed to face. 'It's OK, Tom. The only way you find out answers to things is to ask questions. Sometimes, Perdy, adults have to make difficult choices. That's why I'm taking a sabbatical—that's a kind of long holiday—to think about what I want to do next and make a decision.'

Perdy nodded. 'Like Daddy, when he had to decide whether to come here or stay in London.'

There was a long, long pause. Amy glanced at Tom, and said quietly, 'Well, I think he made a good decision. This is the best place in the world to think, when you're walking along the sand and listening to the waves swishing in and the seagulls crying.'

'I'm not allowed to go on the beach on my own,' Perdy said.

'Your dad's absolutely right. Neither was I, at your age—there always had to be at least two of us, so if one of us got into trouble the other could run for help,' Amy said solemnly. 'And we had to pay attention to the tide warning siren—as soon as we heard it, we had to pack our stuff and come straight home. The tide comes in really quickly here, and people have been cut off.'

'Were they drowned?' Perdy asked.

Amy looked at Tom for guidance, and saw his slight nod. 'Sadly, yes, some of them. But the last one was about five years ago, and it was someone who'd completely ignored the siren. As long as you listen to what the coastguards tell you, you'll be fine.' She smiled to take the sting from her words. 'I'm going to cook dinner. I'll call you when it's ready, shall I?'

'That'd be great,' Tom said. 'Perdy, you need to get changed out of your school uniform, honey.'

'Yes, Daddy.' She scampered up the stairs.

Tom looked ruefully at Amy. 'Sorry about the questioning.'

'Not a problem.' Perdy hadn't pushed for details.

But then she made the mistake of glancing at Tom again. Remembering how it had felt when his hand had touched her face, so briefly. And it made her wonder what it would be like if his hand cupped her face properly and his head dipped so his mouth could brush against hers. How his mouth would feel against hers—warm and sweet, or hot and demanding? Something in the curve of his lips told her that Tom would be a passionate lover.

She really had to stop this. Talk about inappropriate. And hadn't they already agreed boundaries?

'I'd better sort dinner,' she said quickly, panic lancing through her, and disappeared into the kitchen.

She'd regained her equilibrium by the time she called Tom and Perdy for dinner.

'This is really nice,' Perdy said. 'I love spaghetti. It's my favourite.'

'Mine, too,' Tom agreed.

This was so much like the times Amy had spent with Colin and Millie. She'd even cooked Millie's favourite meal, acting completely on automatic. All except the ice cream. Forgetting where she was for a moment, Amy said, 'I was thinking about making some ice cream this weekend.'

'Please can I help?'

Perdy had the same brightness in her eyes that Millie used to have whenever Amy had suggested a baking session. The memories put a lump in her throat so she couldn't speak for a moment; but when she glanced at Tom she could see he looked surprised. Clearly Perdy didn't usually ask something like this. Given that they'd had a rough year—and Amy guessed that the little girl had gone into her shell—it would be cruel to knock her back. And yet the idea of sharing a kitchen with the little girl, getting close to her...

Tom came to her rescue. 'Perdy, honey, I'm on duty tomorrow morning, so you won't be here.'

'Am I coming to the surgery with you?'

He shook his head. 'I was going to ring one of your friends' mums to see if you can play there for the morning and maybe your friend could come here and play in the afternoon.'

'But I haven't got any friends,' Perdy said quietly.

'Oh, darling.' Tom scooped her onto his lap and held her close.

Amy could see in his face that he had no idea what to say, that he was too shocked and dismayed to respond.

And she'd been in Perdy's shoes. She knew exactly what it felt like, not fitting in as a kid. How could she possibly stand by and watch the two of them hurting like this, when she could do something to help?

She reached over and took the little girl's hand. 'Sure you do—you have your dad and Buster.' The thought of what she was about to offer made her voice wobble slightly. 'And me. I mean, we don't know each other very well yet, but we both like Buster and we both like ice cream, and that's a start to becoming friends.'

Perdy's eyes were full of tears. 'But you're busy.'

'With Joseph's papers?' No, she was hiding behind them. She shook her head. 'It's up to me when I work on them. Actually, I was going to get some strawberries tomorrow. If your dad doesn't mind, you can come with me to the shops and then we'll make the ice cream. And if he's not home when we've finished, maybe we can do some baking.' Something Millie had loved doing. And Amy had missed that so, so much.

'Can I, Daddy?'

'I…'

Amy could see the doubt in his face. Well, of course: she was practically a stranger. Or was he worried that they were encroaching on her time? Was Perdy's mother a high-flying career woman who was always too busy, never had enough time? She gave him a smile that felt just a bit too quivery. 'As the saying goes, trust me, I'm a doctor.'

He still looked worried, but then nodded. 'Thanks for the offer.'

Given what Perdy had just said, he didn't exactly have any other options. 'Look, I'll give you my mobile number. If you give me yours,' Amy said, 'I can text you to let you know when we get to the strawberry fields and again when we're back here.'

'Right. Thank you.' Tom looked slightly relieved, but still wary.

And Perdy's eyes were full of worry.

Just what had happened to the two of them? Amy wondered. Despite the agreement she'd made with Tom, she needed to know—to make sure she didn't make things worse for Perdy.

Later that evening, when Perdy had gone to bed, Tom came to find Amy in Joe's study. 'Thank you for what you did at dinner,' he said. 'I've met some of her classmates' mums at the school gate and thought one of them, who seems very nice, might help out. But when she said she didn't have any friends…' He still felt sick at the memory. 'I was so shocked I didn't know what to say, how even to begin to comfort her.' He sighed. 'Oh, hell. I've made the wrong decision, bringing her here.'

'Not necessarily—children are more resilient than you give them credit for.'

He frowned. 'Were you a paediatrician? Child psychologist?'

'No, I wasn't. I'm talking from experience.' She paused. 'I'm trying to respect your boundaries, but there's something I need to ask you.'

Yeah. And he knew what it was going to be. 'What's that?' he asked, playing for time.

'I need to know,' she said, 'which topics I need to avoid with Perdy. Anything that's going to bring back bad memories or upset her. I'll try to stick to neutral things—dogs and books and baking—but kids have a habit of coming out with stuff you're really not expecting.'

Just like Amy herself had. And how come she sounded so clued up about kids? The way she'd acted the night before, Tom had thought that she was the type who concentrated on her career and avoided kids because she didn't know how to deal with them. But today she'd offered to do things with Perdy that he knew his daughter would absolutely love—and the way she'd offered, it was as if it was something she was used to doing. 'I'm trying to respect your boundaries,' he said carefully, 'but why did you offer to look after Perdy?'

'Because I'm sharing a house with you, you're clearly in a hole, and I can do something to help.'

He wasn't buying that, and it obviously showed on her face, because she sighed. 'OK. I was like Perdy when I was a kid. I was shy and booky and found it hard to make friends. I was lucky because I had Joe and Cassie and my cousins to help me make friends with the local kids, but she doesn't have anyone her own age. And what goes around comes around, right?'

Tom was sure there was more to it than that, but it made

a kind of sense. This was her way of paying back kind-nesses that people had done for her when she'd been young.

'Look, if you want to ring Joe or Cassie and ask them if it's safe to let me look after her, that's fine by me.'

Tom blew out a breath. 'Which makes me an over-protective father.'

'No. I'm not prying, but I'm guessing that you're all each other has, and I'd be the same in your shoes. I'd need to know for sure that you weren't unstable before I trusted you with my child.' She took her mobile phone from the desktop and offered it to him.

Tom refused to take it. 'So I'm going to ring the senior partner of the practice—the guy I'm standing in for—and ask him if his niece is trustworthy?'

'It's the only way you can be sure,' she said. 'Or ring Marty—I assume he's acting head of the practice while Joe's away?'

'Yes, he is.' Tom sighed. 'I'm sorry. Given who you are, I know I should be able to take this on trust.'

'But if something major happens in your life, you tend to lose your trust.'

That sounded personal—but asking her to elaborate would be pushing the boundaries, and in return he'd have to tell her about Eloise. Absolutely not. 'I'll call Marty,' he said, taking his own phone out of his pocket.

Five minutes later, he ended the call, red-faced. 'He sang your praises. And I feel a complete and utter heel.'

She shrugged. 'If it was the other way round, I'd check you out before I let my child do anything with you.'

'Thank you,' Tom said. 'For understanding. And for helping.'

'Right now,' she said, 'I think you and Perdy could both do with a friend.'

'Yeah.' He could see the sadness in her eyes. And the dark shadows underneath them that told him she slept badly; whatever had made her take a sabbatical was clearly affecting her sleep, too. 'And I think you could do with one, too.'

'So are there any topics I need to avoid?'

The way she was avoiding answering his comment, he had a pretty good idea that she'd be good at evading anything. And Perdy never talked about Eloise, so there was no point in opening that particular can of worms. 'No. And thank you.'

'No worries.'

'I'll, um, let you get on,' Tom said. If he stayed here much longer he'd be tempted to do something really foolish—like kiss her. And that, he thought, would lead to way too many complications. For both of them.

CHAPTER FOUR

On Saturday, Tom came back from the surgery to the scent of baking. Even when Eloise had been off duty, she hadn't been one for domestic stuff; and he was surprised to discover how much he liked this. He closed the front door quietly behind him, and for once Buster didn't skid across the floor to greet him. No doubt the dog was sitting patiently in the kitchen, waiting for treats.

Tom could hear Perdy and Amy talking in the kitchen as they worked and something twisted inside him. He couldn't ever remember Eloise doing that with Amy; she was always too busy with her charity work to listen to her daughter's jokes. But here was Amy, telling the most atrociously corny jokes, and making Perdy laugh. Perdy was chatting away, saying more words right at that moment than he'd heard her say in a week.

If he hadn't heard it for himself, he would never have believed it. Was it because Perdy missed her mother desperately—even though she never talked about her—and needed someone female around to help bring her out of her shell again? Or was it because she recognised a kindred spirit in Amy—someone else who hadn't fitted in that easily as a child?

Then he froze as he heard Perdy ask, 'So were you the same sort of doctor as my dad is?'

'A family doctor? No. I worked in a hospital,' Amy said.

'What sort of doctor were you?'

'A neurosurgeon.'

Tom blinked. Well, that would explain why he'd thought Amy's hands were delicate. To go with her equally delicate work.

'Is that a brain surgeon?' Perdy asked.

'About a third of my work was inside people's heads, yes, but I didn't work just on people's brains. "Neuro" means "nerves",' Amy explained, 'so I used to do a lot of operations involving people's spines and necks, where there are lots of nerves.'

Tom knew he really ought to walk straight in and distract Perdy, stop her grilling Amy, but her next words froze him to the spot.

'My mum was a doctor, too. She was like the ones you see on telly, in the emergency room. Did you know my mum?'

Oh, no. Oh, no, no, no. He'd been so sure that Perdy never talked about Eloise. He shouldn't have taken it for granted; why the hell hadn't he put his pride to one side and warned Amy, given her an idea what to say if Perdy brought up the subject?

'That depends where your mum works,' Amy said lightly. 'There are quite a few hospitals around.'

'She worked at the London City General.'

'I was at the London Victoria,' Amy said. 'And I didn't work that much with the emergency department, so even if we had worked in the same hospital I probably wouldn't have known her. Sorry.'

Did you know my mum?

Tom had a nasty feeling where that question would've

led if Amy's answer had been yes. Had Eloise ever talked
about her daughter at work, the way most people talked
about their children?

He suspected not. Eloise would've talked more about
her work for Doctors Without Borders, tried to encourage
others to give their time and expertise to help those who
needed aid so badly.

It was important work. Vital work. He knew that and he
wasn't for a moment putting her down for being so caring
about the needs of people who had nothing.

But what about the needs of her own daughter?

He didn't think he'd ever be able to forgive Eloise for that.
For putting their child last when she was still so young and
really needed her mother. For not being able to compromise.

'Why do people need operations on their nerves?'
Perdy asked.

'Because they're in pain—often because there's a lump
pressing on their spinal cord or the nerves.'

'So you have to get rid of the lump and make them better?'

'I used to.'

'Why don't you do it now?'

Amy paused. 'I stopped being good at my job. So that's
why I'm taking a break.'

Tom heard the bleakness in her voice, and guessed
exactly what had happened. Amy had burned out. Maybe
she'd lost a patient and couldn't forgive herself for it.

So right now it seemed that she was in as dark a place
as he was.

Part of him wanted to comfort her; yet part of him knew
it would be a mistake. Too much of a risk. He didn't want
to open himself up to anyone again.

Then Buster barked once and bounded out of the kitchen
towards him.

Should he admit that he'd just overheard the conversation? Then again, it would put Amy in a truly awkward position, where she'd feel obliged to explain more than she wanted to. He'd been there himself too often to do that to her. He walked into the kitchen with a smile that wasn't entirely fake. 'Hello. Something smells nice.'

'Daddy!' Perdy rushed towards him and hugged him. He hugged her right back: his precious little girl.

'We made scones,' she said proudly. 'Amy, are they cool enough to eat yet?'

'You tell me, Perdy. You're nearest the rack. Remember how I showed you to check?'

The little girl put her hand just above the scones, near enough to feel the heat radiating from them but not actually touching the surface and risking a burn. 'They're still warm,' she said.

'Warm or hot?'

'Warm,' Perdy decided.

'That's the perfect time to eat them,' Amy said. 'You like scones, don't you, Tom?'

Even if he'd hated them, he would've choked one down to please his little girl. 'Love them,' he said.

Amy spread her hands. 'OK, Perdy, you're in charge.'

Perdy made an elaborate fuss, putting butter and jam in dishes and laying the table with three plates, knives and napkins, then carefully put the scones on a plate and brought them over, gesturing to her father and Amy to sit down.

There was a huge lump in Tom's throat. His daughter had never, but never, done anything like this before. And yet this felt so right.

'Do you like them, Daddy?' Perdy asked, as he took his first bite.

That wariness was back in her eyes. Fear that she

wouldn't measure up. Yeah, and he knew where that came from. He'd seen enough of it in her mother's eyes. 'They're fantastic,' he said. 'Gold-medal standard.'

Amy took a bite of hers. 'I second that. You've made a fabulous job of these.'

Perdy actually glowed with pleasure.

And how little it had taken to make her do that. Half an hour or so of Amy's time and attention, followed by a little praise.

Why hadn't Eloise been able to do that?

He pushed the thought away, not wanting to spoil his own pleasure in the way his daughter was blossoming before his eyes.

'Amy's going to help me make some "unbirthday" cakes tomorrow,' Perdy informed him. 'So I can take them to school and it'll give everyone something to talk to me about.'

'If you don't mind,' Amy added hastily.

'No, I don't mind at all.' Anything that would make his daughter smile and settle into their new life—anything that would help him break through to her—was fine with him. Even if Perdy grew attached to Amy, they all knew she was here only for the summer, not for ever, so it was safe to let Perdy befriend her. And maybe Amy could help him find a way of connecting with his daughter again.

Perdy was actually smiling when Tom saw her into the playground on Monday morning, carrying her 'unbirthday' cakes. And he knew exactly who he had to thank for that smile.

His surgery didn't start for another twenty minutes; on impulse, he went back to Marsh End House. As he'd half expected, Amy was in Joe's study.

'Is everything OK?' she asked from her desk.

'Yes. Can I interrupt you for a quick word?'

'Sure.'

He walked over to the desk. 'I just wanted to say thanks for all you've done with Perdy this weekend. She actually looked happy going in to school today.'

'Give her time. It's always hard to find your place when you're new,' Amy said. 'And if there are some after-school clubs, they'll help her meet people and make friends, too.'

'Yes, you're right,' Tom said. He paused. 'Um, I overheard her talking to you on Saturday. I'm sorry she grilled you.'

Amy shrugged. 'She asked. I'm not going to lie to her. But I'm also not going to dump stuff on her that's beyond her years, if that's what you're worrying about.'

'No, I didn't think you'd do that. It's just…if you ever want to talk about it,' he offered, 'you know where I am.'

'Thanks, but I'm fine.'

He didn't believe a word of it.

Before he could stop himself, he leaned forward and dropped a kiss on her forehead.

Her eyes widened. 'What was that for?'

Because I needed to kiss you. 'For caring. And for listening to my little girl and hearing stuff I couldn't.'

'I…' He could see that she was looking at his mouth. Just as he was looking at hers, wondering how soft her lips were, how she would taste. He found himself swaying towards her slightly, at the same time as she swayed slightly towards him. The next thing he knew, his mouth was brushing against hers, and the light contact made his lips tingle.

He should stop. He knew he really should stop. For both their sakes.

So why did he catch her lower lip between his? Why were her fingers sliding through his hair? Why was her mouth opening beneath his, letting him deepen the kiss?

Time seemed to stop. All he was aware of was the light floral scent she wore, the warmth and softness of her skin against his, the way she was kissing him back.

It had been so long, so long since he'd last felt this attracted to someone. Hunger bubbled through his veins, melting away his common sense and urging him to take this further. Somehow—he really wasn't sure how—he was sitting on the top of the desk in front of her and she was standing between his thighs. His hands were resting against her hips and his fingers were starting to slide beneath the hem of her T-shirt; her fingers were still threaded through his hair and she was kissing him back, a heady mix of desire and sweetness.

When he finally broke the kiss, it took him a while to realise where he was. Then he looked at Amy. Her pupils were huge, her mouth was reddened and slightly swollen, and embarrassment stained her cheeks.

Guilt flooded through him. What the hell had he been thinking? 'I'm so sorry,' he said. 'I shouldn't have done that.'

She shook her head. 'It wasn't your fault. I was there, too.'

His hands were still at her waist and hers were still round his neck. It would be, oh, so easy to lower his mouth to hers again. All he had to do was dip his head slightly...

Tempting. So, so tempting. And so, so wrong. He dragged in a breath. 'Even so, I shouldn't have done it.' Although Amy had travelled to Norfolk on her own and wasn't wearing a wedding ring, that didn't mean she was single. 'It isn't fair to your partner.'

'I don't have a partner,' she said quietly, 'so it isn't a problem.'

Oh. So she was single. Available.

Possibilities bloomed in his head. And then his common sense wilted them again. Amy might be single, but it didn't mean that she wanted to get involved with anyone. Right now, he needed to concentrate on his daughter, and keeping her life on an even keel after all the upheaval of the last few months. Besides, Amy herself had admitted that she was in a difficult place right now.

He shook his head. 'This isn't a good idea for either of us. Too many complications.'

'You're right. Absolutely,' she agreed.

He needed to take his hands off her. Now. But his body wasn't working in synch with his brain; his hands stayed exactly where they were, just under the hem of her T-shirt, touching warm, soft skin.

With an effort, he released her; a fraction of a second later, she took her hands away from his neck and took a step back.

'I have to go,' he said. Not because he was being a coward. 'I'm due at the surgery.'

She nodded.

He really had to stop looking at her mouth. And kissing her had been a seriously bad idea, because now he knew what it was like to hold her close—and he wanted more. Much more.

'See you later,' he said, and left.

Amy sank back into her chair, propped her elbows on the desk where Tom had been sitting and rested her chin on her hands. What on earth had she been thinking, kissing him back like that? True, she hadn't felt a pull of attraction like this for a very long time, but Tom Ashby was the worst person that she could possibly have a fling with. Apart from the fact that he'd had a rough time recently and needed someone stable in his life—someone who definitely wasn't her, because right now her head was all over the place—he was also a single father. And her experience with Colin had taught her that that was a minefield.

She blew out a breath. On Thursday she'd been so clear about it: don't get involved. And then what had she done? Spent the weekend with them. She'd baked with Perdy, just the way she once had with Millie. Enjoyed watching some of the shadows fade from Perdy's and Tom's faces.

She'd got involved.

Stupid, stupid, stupid.

And yet how could she possibly have stood by and watched them struggle? Perdy's little face on Friday night when she'd said that she had no friends, the distress in Tom's eyes and that lost look on both their faces... No way could Amy have turned her back on them.

But no way could she let herself get any more deeply involved than this.

For the last ten years, work had been everything to her, so the wreckage of her career had left a huge hole in her life. It really wasn't fair to Tom to use him to fill that gap.

If she could catch him later in the day, before Perdy came home, she'd talk to him about it. Explain to him that this morning had been an aberration for both of them—that neither of them was in a position to do anything about the attraction between them right now, and they were both adults so they should be able to treat each other as if they were colleagues.

She damped down the flicker of desire, opened the first of Joseph's casebooks and began to transcribe its contents.

'I really can't handle any more of the pain, Doctor,' Mrs Cooper whispered. 'The drugs just aren't working.'

Tom checked her notes. Mrs Cooper had been complaining of severe pain on the right side of her face, in her cheek, teeth and gums. The dentist had taken X-rays and said the pain wasn't caused by a dental problem, and Joe Rivers had diagnosed trigeminal neuralgia six weeks ago: a condition where the sheath protecting the nerve became damaged, so the lightest touch caused the nerve to send messages of severe pain to the brain.

'I see that Dr Rivers prescribed you some medication,' he said. The usual first-line treatment was anticonvulsants, originally developed to treat epilepsy but found to be useful in treating trigeminal neuralgia. 'Can I just check that you have been taking it regularly?'

She nodded. 'Dr Rivers told me they didn't work like painkillers and I had to take them all the time, not just when I felt the pain. He said we'd wait until I was free of the pain for three weeks, and then we'd start to taper it down to the right dose for me. But it just hasn't worked. And it—' She broke off, scrabbled in her handbag for a pack of tissues, sneezed into one, and then winced, clearly in pain. 'This time of year, it's always bad.'

'Hay fever definitely doesn't help,' Tom said sympathetically. The slightest movement, even a gentle breeze, could cause shooting pains for someone with trigeminal neuralgia; the uncontrollable sneezing that went with hay fever must be agonising. 'I can do something about the hay fever, but I'll need to refer you to the neurology department for more help. As medication hasn't worked, they're likely to suggest surgery to stop the nerve sending pain messages.'

'I don't want to go into hospital.' Her eyes widened with fear. 'I know it's stupid, but my aunt went in for a hip operation last year and she ended up catching that sickness bug. It set her back for months and now we've had to put her in a care home because she can't manage on her own. Before she went in, she was absolutely fine.'

'I'm sorry your aunt had such a bad experience,' Tom said gently, 'but it doesn't mean that you will. For a start, this is summer, so it's very unlikely you'll come into contact with that particular bug. Besides, depending on what kind of surgery they suggest, you might be able to be treated in Outpatients rather than having to stay in for a couple of days.' Given that Amy was on sabbatical, he knew it wouldn't be fair of him to ask her to come and have a chat with his patient. Though Mrs Cooper was clearly suffering from her condition and anxious about the possible treatments, and, as her GP, Tom needed to give her as much help and support as he could. So maybe she would at least talk to him about the possible treatments. 'I might know someone who can give me some more information about exactly what to expect and if there are any other alternatives to surgery,' he said.

'Really?'

'I can't make any promises, but I'll have a word with her and see what I can find out. But in the meantime, let's try a different drug to see if that helps.' Sometimes antidepressants worked where anticonvulsants didn't. He sorted out a prescription and talked her through the medication change. 'We'll need to reduce the dose of your other prescription gradually—if you stop taking it all at once, you're likely to get some nasty side effects.' He wrote down the doses she needed to take for the next week. 'Come and see me this time next week so I can see how you're doing, but give me a ring if it gets any worse.' He flicked into the computer to schedule another appointment, and wrote it down for her. 'I'll refer you to the neurology department as well, because we might as well get the ball rolling—I don't want you to have to wait in pain any longer than you have to.'

'Thank you, Dr Ashby. I'm so sorry to make a fuss.'

'You're not making a fuss at all. This kind of pain's pretty nasty and you're doing really well to cope with it as long as you have. I'll do my best to help you beat this,' he said softly, and her eyes filled with tears. He reached over to squeeze her hand. 'Try not to worry.' And he'd talk to Amy tonight.

About his patient.

And the other problem they needed to sort out.

Tom clearly went straight from his surgery to doing house calls and then the school run, Amy thought, because she didn't see him again until half-past three. She'd just made herself a mug of coffee when Perdy ran into the kitchen, positively glowing, and gave her a huge hug. 'Thank you for making cupcakes with me, Amy. Everyone said they were really scrummy! And Alexis has invited me to tea on Wednesday. Can I ask her to tea here on Thursday, please?'

'Better ask your dad. It's his decision.'

'If he says yes, can we make some more cakes?'

So much for not getting involved. Faced with Perdy's earnest, shy smile and seeing the little girl begin to blossom...how could she say no? Amy smiled back at her. 'Sure we can.'

She glanced at Tom; his expression was slightly dazed, and then she realised where he was looking.

At her mouth.

Was he remembering that kiss this morning?

The thought of it still made her blood heat and desire coil in her belly. And she really hoped she wasn't blushing. 'Tom, what do you think about Amy having her friend over on Thursday? It's my turn to cook, but I don't mind if it's OK with you. As long as I know what Alexis does and doesn't like to eat, that is.'

'Sure.' He still didn't look particularly with it. 'Um, can I have a quick word with you a bit later?'

'No problem,' she said, trying to sound casual, but her heart rate had speeded up.

She knew exactly what he was going to talk to her about. That kiss.

In London, maybe she would've suggested having a mad affair to get it out of their systems. But here it was different; it was a small community, where people noticed what was going on, and Tom had Perdy to think about. So, however strong the attraction between them, they couldn't act on it.

She'd just have to keep taking cold showers and reminding herself that she didn't need the added complication of a love life—she was meant to be using this time to think about her future and what she wanted to do.

CHAPTER FIVE

AFTER Tom had checked that Perdy was settled in bed and kissed her goodnight, he headed downstairs. He could hear a piano playing softly; he followed the sound to discover Amy reading in the conservatory with the stereo on.

'I like this. What is it?' he asked.

'Einaudi. I love the simplicity and elegance.'

'It reminds me of the sea,' he said.

She smiled. 'Not surprising. It's called "*Le Onde*"—The Waves. The first time I heard it, it reminded me of walking on the beach here on a calm summer evening, with the waves lapping at the shore.'

'I was just going to get myself a glass of wine. Would you like to join me?' he asked.

'Thanks, that'd be nice.'

He could see the wariness on her face and knew it was because he'd asked her to have a quick chat with him. Did she think he was going to bring up this morning? They'd have to talk about it at some point, he knew, but right now he wanted to pick her brains about Mrs Cooper—and he had a feeling that was going to be just as awkward a subject. If you'd had enough of your job, to the point where you were taking an open-ended sabbatical, the last thing you'd want to do would be to discuss it. So it would be mean of him to ask.

Then again, wouldn't any doctor in his shoes do the same thing—put their patient's needs first?

'Back in a tick,' he said. He poured two glasses of pinot grigio from the bottle he'd left chilling in the fridge and took them back to the conservatory.

Amy accepted the glass with a smile and took a sip. 'This is very nice.'

'My vice,' Tom said. 'The occasional glass of decent wine.'

She laughed. 'Not like in your student days, when you'd drink anything going?'

He pulled a face. 'Thanks for making me feel middle-aged. I'll have you know, I'm thirty-four.'

'Same as me. Yeah, you're middle-aged,' she teased.

But despite her bantering tone, she looked strained.

Guilt flooded through Tom and his chest felt tight. Was he just about to make everything worse for her? And yet...maybe it would help her to talk. 'There was something I wanted to talk to you about. Given that I'm trying to stick to boundaries, this is probably breaking the rules,' he warned.

Amy was silent for so long that he was about to apologise and offer to leave her be, then she nodded. 'Go on.'

'If you had a patient, say,' he suggested, 'and it was a tricky case, and you had the chance to talk to someone who wasn't going to be involved in your patient's treatment but had much more expertise in that particular area than you did...would you take it?'

She blinked. 'You want to talk to me about work?'

He nodded. 'I know I'm asking a lot. But my patient is worried sick and I want to reassure her—properly, I mean, so she doesn't think I'm just being bright and breezy and fobbing her off. I have no idea whether you know her, but

I'm not going to tell you who she is or give you enough detail to work it out for yourself, so I'm not infringing patient confidentiality. And I could really do with some advice.'

'Uh-huh.'

He could see the struggle in her face. The doctor in her wanting to help, and yet the woman who was on sabbatical not wanting to talk about anything to do with work. 'Amy, if you'd rather not, I do understand—it's not a problem. I don't want to make you feel uncomfortable.'

'But you need to help your patient.' She bit her lip, clearly torn; like him, then, it seemed she'd gone into her profession to help people and make a difference to their lives. 'I'm not sure how much use I can be but, OK, tell me about her.'

'She's in her fifties, and has pain in her right cheek and upper jaw that she describes as feeling like an electric shock,' he said. 'The lightest touch makes it hurt and it doesn't help that she has hay fever—every time she touches her nose or sneezes she's in pain. She's had X-rays from the dentist and everything's fine there.'

'Sounds like a classic presentation of trigeminal neuralgia,' Amy said. 'Though it could be neuritis, especially if she's a diabetic. Is the pain constant?'

'She says it's not—and she's not diabetic,' he explained. 'She's been on anticonvulsants for the last six weeks and it hasn't touched the pain; and she tells me she's taken them properly, not treated them as if they were painkillers, so it isn't that either. I'm referring her to the neurology department for tests. She's a bit nervous about hospitals, so I wanted to know what the procedures are so I could run through them with her beforehand and give her an idea of what to expect.'

'Without actually seeing her myself,' Amy said, 'I can't

say what kind of treatment I'd recommend, but the neurologist will send her for an MRI scan to check if there's an obvious cause for the pain—a tumour, or pressure on the nerve from a blood vessel—and run some tests to rule out any other diseases.' She set her glass down and shifted in her chair so that she was sitting cross-legged. 'Do you know if she's had shingles?'

'It wasn't in her notes,' Tom said.

'It's worth checking, because that's a possible cause,' Amy said. 'Poor woman. I've known cases where the pain was brought on by brushing teeth, or even by going outside on a cold night.'

This was something Tom had missed deeply; he and Eloise had studied together as undergraduates, and he'd loved discussing medicine with her. He'd still been able to discuss things with his colleagues, but it wasn't the same as relaxing after dinner and talking about medicine.

Amy must have enjoyed doing something similar at one point, he guessed, because right at that moment she looked more animated than he'd seen her before, even than when she'd been baking with Perdy.

'So would we be looking at treating with a rhizotomy or microvascular decompression?' he asked.

Amy grinned. 'Did you look it up, or do you know the stuff already?'

'Looked it up,' he confessed. 'I've only come across one case of TGN before.'

'The condition's not that common. It affects roughly one in a thousand men, and two in a thousand women,' Amy said.

'As you told Perdy you were a neurologist, specialising in pain management, I assume you've seen a few?'

'Yes.' She looked thoughtful. 'So your patient is nervous about hospitals. You might have trouble persuading her into microvascular decompression, then, because it's open surgery under a general anaesthetic.'

'So she'd be in for a few days afterwards.'

Amy nodded. 'It can be a good bet because it works for around ninety-five per cent of patients, and ten years later three-quarters of them are still pain-free—though they do get headaches and nausea for a few days after surgery. The operation's still a pretty big deal.' She shrugged. 'Mind you, so's the pain. If she wants to know exactly what happens, we make a cut behind her ear, open the covering of her brain to expose the trigeminal nerve, and then move all the blood vessels and arteries that are compressing the nerve and making it hurt.'

Tom could've listened to Amy all day. She knew what she was talking about, got straight to the point, and didn't try to dress things up to make herself look important. 'What other options are there?'

'A nerve block. We can do that as a day case, and it's much lower risk than microvascular decompression.' She pulled a face. 'But it's still not going to be a pleasant experience. It's done under sedation, so she won't remember much about it afterwards, but the op itself is a bit scary.'

'How scary?'

'Basically I'd put a needle through her cheek under local anaesthetic so it's just inside the skull by the nerve, and then wake her up just enough so she can tell us when the needle touches the nerve in the place where it corresponds to the pain site.'

Tom could imagine explaining that to Mrs Cooper—and he knew she'd hate the idea. 'And it's going to hurt.'

'Briefly, yes. Otherwise I'd work on the wrong part of the nerve and she'd end up still having the pain as well as having to deal with numbness in her face. Once I know which part of the nerve I'm working on, my patient would be back under sedation so she wouldn't be aware of what I'm doing. That's when I'd deaden the nerve—either by injecting glycerol, or using radiofrequency.'

'You're right, it's a scary procedure,' he admitted. 'That'd be tough for anyone to deal with, let alone someone who's terrified of hospitals.'

'And it might need to be repeated,' Amy told him. 'The pain relief lasts from a couple of months through to a couple of years. It leaves the face feeling numb, and some people find that hard to deal with.'

'And that's it? Deadening the nerve under sedation, or open surgery?'

'There's a third possibility,' she said. 'Gamma knife.'

'Which is?'

'A radiation beam, based on cobalt,' she explained. 'It destroys the nerve, and that sorts the problem.'

'It's really not something I've come across,' Tom admitted.

She spread her hands. 'You're a GP. You can't be expected to have in-depth knowledge of every single condition and its treatment. That's why you refer patients to specialists.' Her tone was matter-of-fact but she was smiling, and the tightness in his chest eased.

'Would you mind talking me through it?' he asked.

'Sure. Again, some of it sounds scarier than it really is. First of all, I'd need to attach a metal frame to the patient's skull with pins. The frame's really important because it stops her head moving during the scan and the treatment, and it also means we can be precise about where we're going to direct the radiation beam. It's a bit like the difference between someone taking a photograph at a slow shutter speed and getting a blurred picture, or someone using a tripod so the camera doesn't move and the picture's really sharp.'

Tom liked the way her mind worked; she'd explained it in a way that a layman could understand really well. The sort of specialist he'd be delighted to refer a patient to. 'Does the frame hurt?'

'Yes and no. It feels a bit strange, but it's not heavy, and we'd put a local anaesthetic under the skin at the places where it's pinned—it's no more painful than, say, an injection at the dentist.'

'What happens next?'

'We do an MRI scan, so we can plan the treatment. Then the patient has a break while we look at the scans and work out where the radiation's needed to treat the nerve and how many shots we need to fill that area. We make some final checks then take them into the treatment area. It doesn't hurt and it isn't noisy like an MRI scan is; and if the patient wants to listen to music, we can arrange that.

'What happens after the treatment?'

'We remove the frame and take the patient to the ward for a rest. They might have a bit of a headache and feel tired afterwards, but that's usually from tension rather than the result of the radiation. Some people get a little bit of swelling at the pin sites where the frame's attached, but that goes down in a couple of days.'

'And it's safe for anyone?' Tom asked.

'It's painless, you don't have the risks of an anaesthetic or the risk of haemorrhage or infection that you do from surgery, and the patient can go back to normal activities the next day. So the short answer is yes—but it's still a fairly new procedure, so we don't have any long-term results.'

'If it's new, do I assume that not many centres offer it yet?'

'Not yet,' she admitted.

'Did you use it?' he asked, suddenly curious.

She nodded. 'Last summer, I did a stint with the radiotherapy team, because it's kind of cross-discipline. They use it mainly for treating tumours, but it's also used for movement disorders and for intractable pain, like TGN.'

'So you treated adults rather than children.'

She took a deep breath. 'Sorry, Tom, I'd rather not go there.'

He'd pushed her too far. Time to backtrack swiftly. 'Sorry, my fault. I didn't mean to press you. And thank you for talking to me—I can put my patient's mind at ease now.'

'That's good.'

'And I have to admit, I enjoyed talking medicine with you. I've missed being able to do that.' It was more of an admission than he should've made, he knew, because Amy looked tense again. 'Sorry. I guess I'd better leave you in peace.'

She shook her head. 'I'm not pushing you away. It's just....' She sighed. 'Look, I'm not going to dump my problems on you.'

'That's what friends are for,' Tom said softly. 'I know we don't know each other very well yet, but I think we could be friends.'

She gave him a loaded glance. 'Just friends.'

Yes, he was attracted to her. Very. But he wasn't going to act on it. It wouldn't be fair to anyone. And if he agreed with her now...then that would save them having to have a seriously awkward conversation about that kiss. Maybe then they could pretend it hadn't happened. Retreat into safety. And he could take cold showers to dampen any inappropriate thoughts about how much he'd like to kiss her again. How much he'd like to touch her, feel her touching him. 'Just friends,' he confirmed, lifting his glass. 'Here's to you and me. And friendship.'

'You, me and friendship,' she echoed, lifting her own glass.

CHAPTER SIX

AFTER their agreement on friendship, things settled down. Amy still found herself looking at Tom and wondering what it would feel like to kiss him again, but she kept herself in check. It was the wrong time for both of them. Maybe if they'd met in other circumstances, things would have been different, but, here and now, she knew that friendship was all they could offer each other.

Perdy's friend Alexis came over after school on the Thursday; they made white choc-chip cookies to have with home-made strawberry ice cream for pudding, and Amy was surprised by how much she enjoyed the domesticity of it all. In London, she never had time to bake or potter around in the kitchen; and it was just as well her flat didn't have a garden or it would be overgrown with weeds. Whereas, here, she found that she actually enjoyed twitching weeds out of Cassie's garden and watering the tomato plants in the greenhouse.

It was odd to think that, had things been different ten years ago, her life might have been more like this. She might have been living in Boston or maybe back in London, but she wouldn't have gone home to an empty flat every night. She would've come home to a family. Even if she did love her flat and it was in a smart riverside development, she had to face the fact that it was still empty.

She'd pinned everything on her career. And now that was over...what did she have left?

Maybe her boss was right, she thought wryly, and she did need counselling.

Perdy and Alexis were playing in the garden and Amy was about to call them in for a drink when she overheard Alexis ask, 'So is Amy your mum, then?'

Uh-oh—she really should've asked Tom how he normally dealt with questions, so she could step in and protect his little girl.

But Perdy seemed matter-of-fact as she answered. 'No, my mum caught a fever and died last year when she was helping sick people in Africa.'

So it wasn't a divorce. It was much, much more final than that. Amy's heart bled for her. How did you get over that kind of loss, at such a young age? But there wasn't a catch of pain in the little girl's voice; it sounded as if she'd come to terms with things. Perdy seemed a lot more resilient than Amy herself felt right now. Or Tom, for that matter.

'Oh. So you haven't got a mum,' Alexis said.

'No, but it's OK. She never used to be around much anyway. Dad's cool,' Perdy replied. 'He tells the best bedtime stories.'

Amy stored that away to tell Tom later, when Perdy was asleep, knowing he'd appreciate the compliment. And maybe it might help to heal him.

'So is Amy your dad's girlfriend?' Alexis asked.

Amy froze. Had Alexis heard some kind of gossip in the town, or was she just asking a child's direct question?

But Perdy didn't seem in the least bit fazed. 'No, she's our friend. We met her last week. Her aunt and uncle own the house and she's come to stay for a bit to help us look after Buster.'

'That's cool,' Alexis said, stooping to rub the dog's tummy. 'I wish I had a dog.'

'We couldn't in London because our garden was too tiny,' Perdy confided. 'But Buster's brilliant. Did you know he does proper tricks? Amy showed me.'

Amy relaxed, glad that the conversation was back onto less difficult topics, and went out to ask if the girls wanted a drink, pretending that she hadn't overheard a thing.

Later that evening, when Perdy was in bed, she told Tom what she'd overheard, while being careful not to cross the boundaries and offer him sympathy on the loss of Eloise—or to make a comment about Eloise's parenting skills. She had a feeling that Tom had had more than enough of sympathy—just as she had, after Colin.

'Ouch. So you were right about the grapevine.'

'No, I think it was just an obvious question for a little girl wondering who I was and where I fitted into things,' she said. 'But that wasn't why I told you. I thought you'd like to know that Perdy's clearly very proud of you. So even if you don't think you're doing a good job, she thinks you are.'

'Thank you for that,' Tom said. And she could see in his eyes how much it warmed him.

Over the next few days, Amy and Tom fell into a routine of talking in the conservatory over a glass of wine in the evenings, watching the sky darken and the stars come out. Tom was careful not to ask her anything more about her job, though he did tell her that Mrs Cooper was feeling a lot more reassured. Instead they discussed medicine as it had been in Joseph's time.

'Can you imagine?' Amy asked. 'No anaesthetics, no antiseptics—the pain those poor patients must have gone through. And the only way you could operate on them was to get them completely drunk.'

'Meaning they would've woken up afterwards with the most horrible hangover as well as the pain from the operation,' Tom said. 'I'm glad we don't have to do that nowadays.' He paused. 'So was Joseph a family doctor or a surgeon?'

'A surgeon,' Amy confirmed. 'There's a bit in one of his earlier diaries about how he learned from one of the surgeons who'd been involved with the Resurrection men.'

Tom blinked. 'The body snatchers, you mean?'

She nodded. 'I know it's shocking, but I can understand it. Before the Anatomy Act of 1832, students could only dissect bodies of convicted criminals—and obviously as medicine grew as a discipline, demand outstripped supply. Joseph studied under Sir Astley Cooper. I think that's how he met my great-great-great-great-grandmother, actually, because Astley Cooper came from around here. She'd been invited to one of his parties in London in her debutante year.'

'Small world,' Tom said. 'It sounds fascinating. So what are you going to do with his casebooks? Get them published?'

'Transcribe them, for now, then talk to Dad and Joe and see what they think we should do. Though bits of me would love to write his biography. The way he talks about trying to learn more, wanting to find new ways of helping people…it's inspiring.' And it had reminded her, too, of how much she'd wanted to be a doctor.

Until the operation that had gone so badly wrong and wiped out her confidence.

'So has there always been a doctor in your family ever since Joseph?' Tom asked.

'Every generation,' Amy confirmed. 'Most of us have been surgeons, too; Joe bucked the trend by becoming a family doctor.' She ignored the fact that she would have bucked the trend, too, if she'd continued with her original studies. 'Dad's a cardiac specialist; Granddad was a general surgeon, and so was his father. I never met him, but I do know he served as a medic in the First World War. And one of my great-whatever uncles was at the Crimea.'

'I bet his casebooks would be fascinating. Heart-breaking, but fascinating,' Tom said.

He looked as if he was about to ask why she'd chosen neurosurgery as her specialty, and she swiftly changed the subject to avoid the awkwardness. 'Have you had a chance to explore the coast yet?'

'Not really.'

'The beaches stretch for miles and they've been in all kinds of films, and then at Hunstanton there are the famous stripy cliffs. That's where lots of the fossil-hunters go.'

'Perdy would like that. She had a real dinosaur phase when she was five,' Tom said with a smile. 'Every Sunday we had to go to the Natural History Museum to see the dinosaurs.'

Millie had loved dinosaurs, too, Amy thought with a pang. 'They found a mammoth in the cliffs just down the road at West Runton when Beth and I were teenagers. We spent hours on the beach here, trying to find our own mammoth.'

'I take it you didn't?'

'No.' She laughed. 'But it didn't stop us trying.'

Tom suggested it to Perdy, the following morning. 'That'd be so cool!' the little girl said, her eyes widening.

'Want to come with us, Amy?' Tom asked.

The invitation was casual enough, but Amy knew she was already getting dangerously close to them both. Better to put a little distance between them. 'Thanks, but I've been slacking on Joseph's papers, and I did promise Joe.'

It was a feeble excuse, and she knew Tom saw straight

through it. He looked slightly hurt, and he didn't join her in the conservatory that evening, pleading pressure of paperwork—as flimsy an excuse as her own had been. And Amy was annoyed with herself for feeling hurt in turn, when she knew that keeping away from him was the sensible thing to do.

They kept a polite distance until Wednesday morning, when Amy noticed that Tom was wearing an old faded T-shirt and a pair of tracksuit bottoms instead of the suit he usually wore first thing.

'Are you not in surgery this morning?' she asked.

'I'm doing afternoon surgery today—so I'm glad that Perdy's going to Alexis's house after school again today. Saves me having to split myself into two,' he added softly, clearly mindful that his daughter was only upstairs, brushing her teeth.

She remembered the last time Tom had come back to Marsh End House after dropping Perdy off at school. When he'd kissed her.

Oh, for pity's sake, she had to stop this. Be sensible. Hadn't they agreed that they would be just friends?

'I thought I'd take Buster for a run after I've walked Perdy to school,' he said casually.

'Have fun,' she said with a smile, then headed for Joe's study to work on Joseph's casebooks.

Mid-morning, Amy was having trouble deciphering the cramped script—no wonder his copperplate handwriting had deteriorated to a scrawl, she thought, given that his wife had just had twins and his practice was expanding—so she went to fetch her camera from her room. She was pretty sure that, if she took a photograph of the page and magnified it on the computer, she'd be able to work out some of the more illegible words.

But as she stepped onto the landing Tom walked out of the bathroom. Clearly he'd had a shower after taking the dog for a run because his hair was still damp, and he'd changed into jeans and a different T-shirt. She could smell the clean citrusy scent of his shower gel; and without his glasses he looked different. Less vulnerable. Touchable.

Amy had no idea what possessed her to do such a crazy thing. But she found herself reaching up to touch his face, resting her palm against the curve of his cheek. And then Tom moved, turning his face into her hand; she felt the lightest, gentlest pressure of his lips against her skin.

What happened next was a blur, but then she was in his arms, her own arms wrapped as tightly round him as his were around her, and he was kissing her properly. Just as he had the other morning, his mouth sweet and yet hot and demanding at the same time.

She gave in to the need and slid her hands underneath his T-shirt; his muscles were firm and toned and felt like heaven.

And then his hands slid under her own T-shirt, the pads of his fingers moving in tiny circles against her skin. Amy felt as if she was burning up with need and desire; she couldn't remember wanting anyone so badly.

Neither of them could drag their mouth away from the other's for long enough to speak, but by silent consent they both moved towards her room. She knew nobody could see into her room at the back of the house, but all the same she dragged the curtains closed. Who removed whose clothes, she had no idea, but at last they were naked and he was lifting her onto the bed. He kissed his way down her throat; she arched against the bed, offering him more, and he kissed his way down her breastbone, so slowly that it drove her crazy. She slid her hands into his hair and drew him closer, wanting more. His hair was so soft and his mouth was hard and hot, the perfect combination; and then at last his mouth closed round one nipple, teasing it with his tongue and his teeth. She heard herself whimper his name, and he paid similar attention to the other nipple, driving her crazy. He nudged one thigh between hers; if he wasn't inside her in the next five seconds, she knew she was going to implode.

But then he tensed.

And stopped.

'Tom?' Her voice was so ragged she barely recognised it.

He dragged in a breath. 'We have to stop. While I can still think straight.'

What? Why? Her head was all over the place.

'I don't have a condom,' he said.

That was it? The only reason? Relief flooded through her. 'I do. I think,' she added. She really, really hoped she did.

'Thank God—because I feel like a teenager right now, hopelessly unprepared.'

She loved the fact that he admitted it, instead of going for macho posturing and pretending that this was something he did all the time. And there was something about him that made her feel like a teenager, too, full of desire and no idea how to handle it.

She slid off the bed and went to the zipped compartment in her handbag. Please, please let them be there, she begged silently as she opened the zip. To her relief, there was still a small packet of condoms there. And there was one left. She checked the date and blew out a breath. 'Thank God.'

'That you have one?'

'That it's still in date,' she corrected. 'If it hadn't been, I think I might just have imploded.'

'That makes two of us,' Tom admitted, and held his hand out to her.

She took it; he pulled her into his arms and kissed her again. Kissed her until she felt utterly boneless and she couldn't think straight.

She heard him rip the packet, then the unmistakeable sound of the condom being rolled on; and then, at last, he was kneeling between her thighs again, nudging them apart.

Slowly, slowly, he eased into her, giving her time to get used to his weight and the feel of him inside her.

Strange how such an unfamiliar body could feel so familiar. So right. So perfect.

For a moment, she felt as if she'd been waiting for this for her entire life.

But that was insane. Of course she hadn't. This was just mad, crazy desire and this would get it out of their systems—and then they could go back to normal.

Couldn't they?

To stop herself thinking, she kissed him again; he responded, lifting her hips so he could push deeper into her. Right at that moment, the empty space in her life seemed to flatten and fade away; her entire senses were filled with Tom.

Warmth spread through her body, coiling deep inside her, and then suddenly she was falling over the edge. She felt Tom go still as her body rippled round his; clearly he, too, had hit the peak.

When he'd dealt with the condom, he came to sit next to her on the bed. His expression was unreadable, but she had the feeling he was brooding.

'OK?' she asked softly.

'Yes.' He sighed. 'No.' He grimaced. 'Sorry. Boundaries. I'm not going to dump that on you.'

She smiled wryly. 'And didn't we say last week we were just going to be friends?'

'Yes.' He returned her smile. 'I didn't intend it to be a euphemism.'

'Do you regret it?' she asked.

He looked at her, his hazel eyes clear. 'Do you want an honest answer or a tactful one?'

She flinched. 'I think you've just given me your answer.'

He reached across and pulled her close. 'I don't regret making love with you, Amy, because I find you incredibly attractive and I've wanted you since the minute I first saw you.'

'But?' Even though he didn't say the word, it was written all over his face.

He sighed and rested his forehead on her shoulder. 'It's complicated. There's Perdy.'

Oh, yeah. Been there, done that, worn the T-shirt and broken my heart. She really ought to know better than to get involved with a single father. 'Perdy doesn't have to know about this. It's not going to change the way I behave towards her and it's not going to change the way we behave to each other in front of her.'

'Thank you. But I still feel guilty as hell.'

'You said you were single,' she reminded him.

'I am.' He lifted his head again and blew out a breath. 'It doesn't stop me feeling as if I've just betrayed my—' He stopped abruptly.

She could guess the word he hadn't said. 'Was I the first since your...' *Since your wife died.* She couldn't bring herself to say it, either. 'Since Perdy's mother?'

He nodded.

She stroked his face. 'If it helps, the first time afterwards, you do feel guilty as hell. As if you're doing something wrong.'

His eyes widened. 'You, too?'

She shook her head. 'We weren't married.' She took a deep breath. 'But we were going to be.' Maybe if she explained about Colin, Tom would realise that he didn't have to worry—that she wasn't expecting anything from him. 'I was in my pre-reg year as a paediatrician, and Colin was a surgeon. He was ten years older than I was, but the age difference didn't bother either of us.' She dragged in a breath. 'He had a little girl, Millie—she was four when we started seeing each other. He'd split up with her mother a year before, and he had custody of Millie because his ex-wife wanted to pursue her career.'

She saw Tom flinch, and she had a feeling that she'd just hit a nerve. Given what she'd overheard Perdy saying, his wife had clearly been very work-oriented.

'We started dating, and I adored Millie. We got on brilliantly together. He asked me to marry him, and I loved the idea of being part of their family—Millie was delighted, especially as she was going to be our bridesmaid.' She bit her lip. 'When Colin said he wanted to move to America so Millie could at least see some of her mother, I agreed to finish my training in the States. The plan was, he'd go out first, get Millie settled, and then I'd join them.'

Tom's arms tightened round her. 'But it didn't happen?'

She shook her head. 'He'd been out there two months, and I'd given my notice, sold my flat and all my furniture. All I had to do was pack the stuff I wanted to take with me to America.' She swallowed. 'But then he rang me. He said that Millie was so pleased to be with her mother again that he'd had a long talk with his ex and they'd decided to make another go of their marriage. He was sorry, but it was over.'

'Just like that?'

'Completely out of the blue.'

Tom blew out a breath. 'That was seriously rough on you.'

'It knocked me for six. I didn't just lose my partner, I lost the little girl I'd started to think of as my daughter. Colin said he thought it was best if we made a clean break. And I wasn't going to stand in the way of his little girl's happiness.' She shrugged. 'I hope they've been happy. I have no idea, but I really hope they have, for Millie's sake.'

'I don't know what to say,' Tom said. 'Just that I'm sorry he hurt you like that. And I think I understand now why you were wary of Perdy. And why you didn't want to come to the beach with us last weekend.'

Amy nodded. 'I like Perdy. Very much. But I'm…' Not looking to get involved again. Though she couldn't think of a way to put it without hurting Tom. She changed tack. 'I'm trying to tell you I understand how it feels. That I know horrible it is when everyone pities you, and how the first time you even think about dating someone afterwards you feel as if you're cheating on your partner.'

'I've had enough pity to last a lifetime,' Tom said. 'It must've been worse for you, though, being the focus of the hospital grapevine.'

'That's one of the reasons I asked to change specialties as soon as my rotation was over,' she admitted.

'And neurology's a tough discipline. You'd have been too busy studying to—well, even think about Colin and Millie.'

'Exactly.' Neurology was a challenge—something to fill her head and all the empty spaces inside. 'I loved my work. And the fact it kept me too busy to have a serious relationship… Well.' She shrugged. 'I guess that was a bonus.'

'And you've never met anyone you've wanted to…?'

'I've had relationships, yes. But I kept them light. I don't want to get hurt again, Tom. And, just so you know, I'm not looking at you and Perdy as a substitute for Colin and Millie.'

'Thank you. And I'm not looking at you as a substitute for Eloise.' He looked at her. 'So where do we go from here?'

'I don't know.' She bit her lip. 'Tom, I find you really attractive, too. And what happened just now… I need you to know, I'm not in the habit of doing that.'

'Neither am I,' Tom assured her.

'I guessed that.' She took a deep breath. 'I think we both needed it, so we shouldn't beat ourselves up for it.' And now for the big one. 'But I don't think we should repeat it.' Not because she didn't want to, but because she was scared what might happen if they did. It terrified her that she was going to fall in love with Tom and Perdy and her heart would end up broken all over again. 'Neither of us is in a position to start anything. I don't know how long I'm going to be here and you have Perdy to think about.'

'So you regret it?'

'Do you want the honest answer or the tactful one?' she asked, bouncing his question back to him.

'Ah. So that's a yes.'

'It's a yes and a no,' she said. 'Nothing in life's ever that black and white. There's always a shade of grey in there. And neither of us can really deal with this right now.' She pressed a kiss against his chest. 'I need a shower.'

He groaned. 'You've just put a picture in my head. A really inappropriate one.'

One that was now very firmly in hers. Of Tom soaping her all over, touching and tasting and kissing until she was breathless. Lifting her against the wall. Easing his body into hers before taking her back to the edge. 'Tom. This really isn't a good idea,' she warned. 'Those boundaries we agreed on—I think we'd better agree on some additional ones. Physical ones.'

'This isn't going to happen again. We're going to be

sensible,' he said. 'I agree with you—right now, we both needed that. But there are too many complications for us to take this further.'

'OK. So we'll just pretend this didn't happen, and everything will be fine. There won't be any awkwardness between us, for Perdy's sake.'

'Agreed,' he said.

It was the sensible thing to do. She knew that.

But when Tom had pulled on enough clothes to make himself decent, scooped up the rest and left her room without a backward glance, she curled back under the duvet, and wished that things could've been different.

Amy felt even more wistful the following evening, when Cassie called to tell her that Beth's baby had arrived. 'Amy, he's gorgeous. And huge! He was almost four kilos.'

'That's big for a first baby,' Amy agreed. 'How's Beth?'

'She's absolutely fine and completely in love with Sam— Samuel Joseph, that is,' Cassie added. 'He's adorable, Amy. I've taken tons of photos and I'll email you some later tonight. I just wanted to tell you the news myself.'

In a seriously expensive phone call. 'I'd better let you go,' Amy said, 'but give everyone my love, and cuddle the baby for me, OK? Is Beth staying in hospital for long?'

'She's coming home tomorrow,' Cassie said.

'Great. I'll send her something.' It wasn't a late or unplanned decision; Amy had spotted what she wanted to send, a while back, but she hadn't wanted to tempt fate by ordering it before the baby arrived.

Part of her was tempted to fly out to Australia to see the baby for herself. But she knew that that would be running away from the situation with Tom, and she'd already done enough running, fleeing from London. She'd just have to wait it out. Besides, Cassie and Beth would take one look at her and make her spill the whole story, and no way did Amy want to put a dampener on these first few precious days with the baby.

So instead she put a dent in her credit card, organising a bouquet of singing helium balloons to be delivered to Beth's house the next morning, along with a bottle of champagne and a large box of chocolates for the parents and grandparents to enjoy, and a pile of educational toys and a lullaby light show featuring a teddy in a train for little Sam.

And this sudden, unexpected loneliness seeping through her—it would go.

It had to.

CHAPTER SEVEN

SENSIBLE, Tom thought grimly, was overrated.

If he looked at things clearly, then of course he could see that it was sensible not to get involved with Amy. The little she'd said about her job—and the way he'd seen her throw herself into the task of transcribing Joseph's casebook—made it obvious that her career had been the main focus of her life. Just as Eloise's career had been her main focus of her life. At the end of her sabbatical, Amy would go back to London and sort things out and go back to her career—and a life that wouldn't have space for him and Perdy.

His head knew it.

But could he get his body to accept it? No. It tortured him with memories. The softness of her skin. The warmth of her body. The curve of her mouth. Her soft, floral scent. The little noises of pleasure she'd made as he'd pushed deeper into her. The way he'd actually felt a kind of peace as he'd lost himself inside her.

It was driving him crazy.

Cold showers didn't help. Neither did taking Buster for a run, even if he took his MP3 player and played classic rock at high volume through his headphones. It left him energised instead of exhausted. Worse still was sitting down with her in the evenings, because he could barely take his eyes off Amy's mouth. Every time she took a sip of wine, he found himself remembering the feel of her mouth against his and had to damp down the longing to put his glass down, take hers from her fingers and kiss her until they were both dizzy.

And he'd caught her staring at his mouth, too.

Was it the same for her? he wondered. Was she lying awake at in the middle of the night, thinking that there were only two closed doors and a landing between them? Remembering how good it had felt to be with each other, no barriers between them? Remembering the warmth of his skin against hers?

There was no respite at the weekend either, because even though Amy didn't come on a trip out with them on the Saturday—she'd pleaded a headache that he was pretty sure was convenient rather than real—Perdy didn't stop talking about her. And on Sunday Amy joined them for a walk on the beach, helping Perdy look for shells and interesting stones; seeing her walk barefoot on the sand stoked his desire higher still. She had beautiful feet, narrow and graceful. Her toenails were painted a silvery rose colour—nail polish that his daughter was also sporting on her toes, he noticed. And she wore a ring on the second toe of her right foot, in a complicated Celtic swirl design. It made him want to touch. Explore. Discover her sensitive spots, the places where she liked being touched and kissed, what made her eyes go unfocussed.

And if this went on for much longer, he'd go insane.

By Tuesday morning, tension was thrumming through him. And when he got back from the school run to discover a letter from Eloise's parents—a letter that they'd sent to his house in London, despite the fact that he'd told them

where he and Perdy would be for the next few months—
he started grinding his teeth.

The dictat that he should bring Perdy to visit them was
the final straw. He banged his mug of coffee down on the
table and swore. Loudly.

Buster came bounding into the kitchen and put his head
on Tom's knee, as if checking that he was all right.

And a few moments later Amy stood in the doorway,
one eyebrow raised. 'What's happened?'

'Eloise's parents, that's what!' He dragged in a breath.
'They're so bloody high-handed, it's untrue. They're demanding I take Perdy to see them this weekend. As if it's
perfectly reasonable for them to expect me to drop everything, cancel any plans I'd made, and drag her off to
Chester at a couple of days' notice.'

'Maybe they'd like to see their granddaughter,' Amy
suggested.

'Yeah, right—which is why they never phone her,
never write to her or send her a little card just to say hello
and let her know they're thinking about her. Do you know,
they actually sent this to London instead of here?' He
shook his head in annoyance and frustration. 'I gave them
all our contact details well before we left London. And
they have my mobile number. So why couldn't they get
in touch and talk to me like normal people, instead of
issuing a bloody decree?'

Without comment, Amy took the cake tin out of the
cupboard, cut a large slice of chocolate cake, put it on a
plate and slid it in front of him.

'What's this?'

'Anger management,' she said. 'Don't say a word. Eat
this and count to a hundred in your head. And then talk.'

'I don't need ang...' He let the words trail away, and

sighed. 'I'm sorry. You're right. I'm ranting and raving, and it's not fair to dump this on you.'

'It's OK. Everyone has bad days.'

'I'm just glad Perdy wasn't here to see any of that. Or hear it. I'm not perfect, by any means, but I do try not to swear in front of her.' He bit his lip. 'Or anyone female, for that matter. It's not how I was brought up. I owe you an apology for that.'

'Maybe,' Amy suggested, 'talking about it might help.'

He was about to argue when she added, 'How many patients do you tell not to bottle things up because it's bad for their blood pressure?'

'Point taken. I'm being a hypocrite.'

She smiled. 'At least you know it. Eat your cake, count to a hundred, and I'll make us both a coffee—seeing as half of yours ended up over the table.'

He shook his head. 'It's my mess. Give me a cloth and I'll sort it.'

'Just shut up and eat your cake,' Amy said, and deftly removed all evidence of the spill before he could protest.

By the time he'd eaten the cake and counted silently to a hundred, she'd made coffee. She placed a fresh mug in front of him then sat opposite. 'OK. Talk to me.'

He shook his head. 'It's not going to change anything.'

'It won't change the past,' she said, 'but it might help you see it differently so you can deal with it more easily.'

He was silent for so long that she thought he was going to refuse. Eventually, he nodded. 'Just promise me you're not going to pity me,' he said. 'I've had enough pity to last me for the rest of my life.'

'I won't pity you,' Amy promised.

'Thank you.' Tom wrapped one of his hands round the mug of coffee. 'Eloise's parents were high flyers, so she always felt she had to live up to them and do better than anyone else.'

Amy nodded. She knew exactly how Tom's late wife had felt—that was one of the things that had driven her choice of career, too. Wanting to do what every generation of her family had done for nearly two hundred years. Wanting to be as good as her parents were.

'I met her at university. She was top of our year.' He smiled wryly. 'I admit, she was vying with me for the top spot. That's how we got together in the first place—I don't think she would have noticed me otherwise. But when you want to be the best, you notice anyone who's a potential rival.'

'Women tend to notice men for other reasons, Tom. Trust me on that,' she said. She'd definitely noticed him for other reasons than his mind—though that attracted her, too.

'I wasn't fishing.' Colour stained his cheeks. 'I suppose what I was trying to say is Eloise wanted to tell her parents that she'd graduated top of her year and was on a fast track to becoming a consultant. Perdy wasn't planned; we'd only just both qualified when Eloise realised that she was pregnant.' He bit his lip. 'I was thrilled—I'd always expected that we'd have children, and as far as I was concerned it simply meant that we'd started our family a bit earlier than we'd planned. But Eloise was terrified that it meant the end of her career. I suppose it was hard for her: telling her parents that she was pregnant and getting married seemed like being a failure, in her eyes.'

Amy frowned. 'Why? Why couldn't she have a career and you and Perdy?'

'That's how I saw it,' Tom said grimly. 'But Eloise felt she'd failed. That was why I switched from paediatrics to training as a GP: it meant my hours would be more regular than if I worked on a ward, and I could take care of Perdy while Eloise worked the hours she needed to get on in her career.' He shrugged. 'I suppose you could say we switched roles. She was the one with the huge career, and I was the one who sorted out the family side of things.'

'Has it occurred to you,' Amy asked, 'that that's a strength? You were the one holding everything together. Like a human pyramid. Sure, there's someone at the top—but without a strong base, the whole thing collapses.'

'My point exactly. We collapsed because I couldn't give her the base she needed. Before we qualified, she always planned to work for Doctors Without Borders, the way her parents had done when they'd first qualified. And I could see it was eating away at her that she hadn't done it.' His eyes were full of misery. 'I thought maybe if she went out and spent maybe a couple of weeks a year working for them, it would make her feel that she made a difference and she'd stop resenting me for trapping her in domesticity.'

'Did it?'

Tom shook his head. 'It still wasn't enough. And it's my fault that she died. If I hadn't suggested she did a stint every year, she wouldn't have gone to Africa. If she hadn't gone to Africa, she wouldn't have caught a tropical fever. And if she hadn't caught the fever, she wouldn't have died.' He ticked the points off on his fingers, and Amy could see the guilt and misery in his eyes.

'There's another way of looking at this,' she said softly. 'If you hadn't let her go, she would've resented you for it. And she probably would have left you and Perdy anyway, gone out there full time. There's always a risk when you're working in an area with serious infectious diseases, and everyone who goes out there knows that and accepts that risk. It's not your fault. It was her decision to go, Tom. You didn't push her into it.'

'Maybe not.' He sighed, the sadness expanding inside him. 'Ah, hell. It's been a year, and I still can't deal with it. I miss her—of course I miss her—and it's so hard bringing up Perdy without having someone to talk to, someone who can help me sort out the problems before they get too huge. But I'm so angry with her at the same time. Perdy and I just weren't enough for her, and I just can't forgive her for that.'

'How can you be so sure you weren't enough for her?'

Tom sighed. 'She wasn't happy, right from when we found out she was pregnant. She had really bad morning sickness at the start—and as soon as that stopped, the indigestion started. She hated being pregnant. And during labour she told me she wished she'd never got pregnant.'

'So I hear, a lot of women say that sort of thing during labour,' Amy said. 'Didn't your midwife warn you not to take transition talk seriously?'

'It went deeper than that,' Tom said. 'She never really bonded with Perdy. I did wonder at first if Eloise might have postnatal depression, but then I realised it wasn't that. It was just how Eloise was, the way she'd been brought up. She just didn't know how to love our baby. And I think Perdy knew it, too—she never talks about her mother. Ever.' He bit his lip. 'It worries me that she's bottling it all up, but I don't know how to get her to talk to me about it.'

'People deal with things in different ways,' Amy said softly. 'Not talking about it to you doesn't necessarily means she's bottling it up. She might talk about it to someone else.'

'Why not me? I'm her dad.'

Amy could see the hurt in his eyes. She kissed him lightly. 'Maybe she thinks it hurts you too much to talk about her—and talking to someone else means that she won't be hurting you.'

He sighed. 'I just wish I could be sure that she's OK.'

'Hey. Parents are supposed to worry about their kids.' Amy ruffled his hair.

'Eloise never seemed to worry about her. Not the way I do.' He sighed. 'I suppose she was just following her parents' lead. I could never quite understand them. I mean, I'm an only child too and my parents have always loved me to bits. They were so proud of me, and I always knew it didn't matter if I didn't come first, as long as I'd tried my hardest. I knew that coming second didn't mean they wouldn't love me. But Eloise… If she didn't come top, her parents weren't interested. And I never saw them show any affection towards her—all they were interested in was how she was doing at work, when she was going to get a chance for promotion.'

'What about Perdy? She's their only grandchild.'

'Yes, and you'd think they'd have been thrilled about it. But even when they saw Perdy for the first time, they didn't give Eloise a huge hug and tell her how gorgeous the baby was or any of the stuff normal grandparents would say, whereas my parents fell in love with Perdy from the very second they saw her. They always greeted us with a hug and a kiss, and before Dad's arthritis got bad he always used to carry Perdy around on his shoulders and get down on the floor to play games with her. Eloise's parents never did anything like that with her. They've never even read her a story or sat colouring a picture with her. They're air-kissers,' he said, looking disgusted.

'So are my parents,' Amy said.

He blinked. 'I would never have guessed. I mean, Joe and Cassie…'

'Are incredibly warm,' Amy agreed. 'But I think Cassie changed Joe. She made him who he is today. My grandfather had a real stiff upper lip, and Dad and Joe inherited it. Being the younger son, Dad felt he had to prove himself— don't get me wrong, he and Joe love each other, but there's a fair bit of sibling rivalry between them. I was a month early, meaning that I'm three days older than Beth, and I can just imagine how much Dad crowed that he'd produced the first grandchild. And my mother always said that there was a glass ceiling—she had to work twice as hard as Dad to get anywhere. So their work's always been their focus in life.'

Tom frowned. 'So your upbringing was pretty much like Eloise's.'

'Let's leave it that what you told me rang a few bells,' Amy said dryly.

'But you're not like Eloise was. I mean, the way you've spent time with Perdy—you've told her silly jokes, you've taught her skipping games, you've shown her how to make the dog do tricks. Eloise would never have done anything like that with her.'

Maybe that, Amy thought, was why Perdy hardly talked about her mother. Because Eloise had been as distant as her own parents had been. And Amy could so, so easily have turned out like that herself. 'She might not have been comfortable playing games or doing messy stuff. Some people aren't. But she did other things with Perdy, didn't she?'

Tom sighed. 'The more I look at it, the less I can see. The less I can remember. She never even made it to Perdy's nativity plays—she got me to video them for her, but it wasn't the same as actually being there in the audience so Perdy could look out from the stage and see her clapping next to all the other mums.' He dragged in a breath. 'I have days when I wonder why the hell I married her—and then I feel guilty about being so mean and judgemental.'

'Feelings aren't all black and white,' Amy said. 'They're

complicated.' Like the way she was feeling right now about Tom. Wanting to preserve some distance between them to keep her heart safe, and yet at the same time unable to keep away. 'If I hadn't had Joe and Cassie, I might've had the same kind of trouble as Eloise—I wouldn't have known how to show people I cared. Joe and Cassie showed me.' She grimaced. 'Don't get me wrong, I do love my parents—but I'm a lot closer to Joe and Cassie than I am to them.'

The pain in Tom's eyes deepened. 'I tried to show Eloise how to love, and I think Perdy tried, too. But we just weren't enough for her. She wanted to save the world, and we were just in the way.' He looked bleak. 'And I resent her for that. I really resent her. What kind of sick bastard am I, to be angry with someone who's dead and can't defend herself?'

'A perfectly human one. It's one of the stages of grief,' Amy said softly.

'It's still wrong of me to feel that way. Eloise did so much good in the world, and it's tragic that she died young. Thirty-three's no age at all.'

'True. But she wasn't able to give you and Perdy what you needed,' Amy pointed out. 'A partnership's about give and take. And you always, always put your child first, no matter what your ambitions and hopes are.' That was what she'd done with Millie. In that situation, someone had had to lose, and it was better that it had been her rather than the little girl. As an adult, she'd had a better capacity to deal with it. Even though it had ripped her heart into little pieces. 'Tom, you've done a fantastic job bringing Perdy up.'

'Have I?'

She knew the self-doubt was real, and that he wasn't fishing for compliments. Clearly he was terrified that his child would grow up with the same emotional blocks as her mother, and he felt powerless to stop it happening.

'Let me ask you something. When Perdy woke in the night as a baby, who went to see her? Who fed her, changed her nappy, rocked her back to sleep?'

'I did,' he admitted, 'because I was the one who was there. Eloise would've done it had she not been on night duty or what have you.'

Amy didn't share his conviction, but kept her thoughts to herself. 'OK, let me ask you something else. Who read her bedtime stories? Who picked her up when she fell over, kissed a bruise better and put sticking plasters over cuts?'

'I get your point.'

'I don't think you do. Tom, what I'm trying to say is that Perdy's not going to be like Eloise. She's grown up with affection in her life. She knows that she's loved. I've seen you with her—you always talk to her about her day and take an interest in what she does, and it's not just focussed on whether she got ten out of ten on her spelling tests. You ask her what she enjoyed best in her day, what she had for school dinner.'

'But she's so quiet, Amy. So quiet and neat and tidy.' He shook his head in seeming frustration. 'It's like she isn't a child.'

'Of course she is,' Amy reassured him. 'Not all kids are messy and noisy and race around all the time. I was always quiet, when I wasn't here—and even here, I was always quiet for the first few days of the holidays, until I'd settled back into being part of Joe and Cassie's brood. Yes, Perdy chatters a bit to me, but I think that's because she recognises me as someone who was the same as her when I was little.' Another thing that had made them bond: they understood each other instinctively. 'Don't judge yourself too harshly, Tom. It's tough, being a single parent. As you said, you don't have anyone to talk over your decisions with. You worry that you're doing it wrong. Anyone would, in your shoes. But you're doing your best—and what you're doing is good enough.'

'It doesn't feel it.'

'Tom, you don't have to be perfect. It's probably better that you're not—because then your child knows life doesn't always work the way you want it to, and you can show by example that there are different ways of dealing with problems.' She smiled at him. 'Perdy believes in you, so give yourself a break and start believing in yourself.' She reached over and squeezed his free hand.

But when she was about to release him, Tom drew her hand up to his mouth and kissed each knuckle in turn. Then, with his gaze locked with hers, he kissed the pulse that beat crazily at her wrist.

She knew she ought to pull away, that this was a bad idea. And yet at the same time, maybe it wasn't. She could comfort Tom, make him feel better. Make him feel loved, the way Eloise hadn't been able to make him feel. And he could drive her nightmares away. Let her feel something other than panic and regret.

She knew these were dangerous thoughts. Ones she didn't have the right to have. But she couldn't stop them.

The feel of his mouth against her skin made her feel as if she were dissolving. She touched his face with her other hand, stroking his cheek. He'd shaved that morning and his skin was soft, warm. Inviting.

'Tom,' she said softly.

He stood up, moved to her side of the table and drew her to her feet. He dipped his head and kissed the corner of her mouth, making her shiver. His mouth brushed lightly against hers—and then they were kissing in earnest. Tom lifted her onto the table and nudged his thighs between hers; she wrapped her legs round his thighs, drawing him closer.

When he broke the kiss, he stared at her. 'I'm so sorry, Amy. That wasn't fair of me. You've been hurt before and I shouldn't try to rush you into...whatever this thing is between us.'

This was her cue to release him and slide off the table.

But she didn't. Couldn't. She simply reached up to run the pad of her forefinger along his lower lip. 'It wasn't just you,' she said. 'And before... I don't think it was enough to get this out of our systems.'

'So what are you suggesting?' he asked.

'Neither of us is in a fit state to consider a relationship. We're both in a bad place,' she said. 'But maybe...' This was a huge risk, and if he turned her down, there was no way she'd be able to stay here. But his eyes held a question—and a tiny flicker of hope.

He pressed a kiss into her palm and closed her fingers over it. 'Maybe what?'

'Maybe...' Oh, why was this so hard to say? 'Maybe we can help each other out of the bad place.'

His eyes turned the most amazing shade of grey-green. Shimmering. Like the sea on a winter afternoon, lit by a pale sun. 'I've been going slowly crazy these last few days—lying awake at night, thinking of you.'

'Me, too,' she said. And it hadn't been the nightmares that had kept her awake the last couple of nights. It had been remembering how Tom had touched her. How he'd felt beneath her fingertips. How his mouth had felt against hers. And how she wanted more.

'I want to make love with you,' he told her, his voice low and fierce and almost cracked with longing. 'Right now. I want to lose myself in you. Let you lose yourself in me.' He brushed a kiss against her mouth. 'But.'

He had objections?

He smiled. 'No objections.'

She felt her face flush. 'Uh. I didn't intend to say that out loud.'

He stole a kiss. 'I know. All I meant was, we're going to have to wait until I can go into the next large town and buy a pack of condoms from someone who doesn't know either of us.'

'If either of us goes into the village to buy some, the news is going to be all around the village before we get home,' she agreed wryly. 'And we've already used my last one.' She reached up to steal a kiss. 'Just so you know, I don't make a habit of this kind of thing.'

'Neither do I.' He kissed the tip of her nose. 'I guess the boundaries have shifted again.'

Yes, and she needed to re-establish them. Put the rules in place so neither of them got hurt. 'This is just between us. For as long as…well. As long as I'm here, as long as we're both hurting.' Because she wasn't staying and she didn't want either of them having any false illusions. 'But as far as everyone else is concerned—including Perdy, because it's not fair to tell her about this until we're sure about whatever's happening—we're just sharing a house and dog-sitting duties.' She paused. 'And I won't repeat what you told me.'

'I know you won't. And I appreciate that.' He smiled. 'I trust you, so I wasn't even going to ask you to keep it confidential.' He drew her close and rested his cheek against hers. 'I've dumped a lot on you. I'm sorry.'

'Don't apologise. Apart from the fact that I dumped all the stuff about Colin on you, the other I asked you to tell me. And I think you needed to get some of that out. To give you space inside to see a different slant on things.' She stroked his hair. 'So what are you going to do about Perdy's grandparents?'

He sighed. 'Ring them and sort out a more reasonable date for a visit. They need to understand that I'm not going to ask "how high" every time they say "jump", and they'll see Perdy only with me—so I can step in if they try pressuring her the way they pressured Eloise. I love my little girl for who she is, not because she's pretty and she's clever. And no way am I abandoning her to their clutches.'

Amy couldn't help smiling. 'Tom, that's a bit dramatic. Don't forget, they lost their only child.'

'And they're not replacing her with mine,' he said grimly.

'Have they challenged you for custody?'

'No.' His eyes widened. 'Oh, my God. That never occurred to me.'

'Tom, they wouldn't have a chance in hell. No court would take a child from where she's very clearly loved and flourishing and put her somewhere else.' She stroked the hair away from his forehead. 'My guess is that they miss Eloise, they've had time to think about the mistakes they've made, and they really want to see Perdy. Except they're hopeless at communicating. And, because of the way they've behaved in the past, you feel defensive—as anyone else in your situation would—and maybe you're reading things into their words that they didn't actually mean.'

'Maybe.' Tom gave her a rueful smile. 'Have you always been this clear-sighted?'

'It's a lot easier to do for other people than for yourself,' she said.

'It's still appreciated, though.' He sighed. 'I admit, I resent Eloise's parents, too. Maybe if they'd put less pressure on Eloise and made her feel more loved, she would've been happy with me and Perdy. She would've been content to have a career and a family, instead of feeling that she had to excel at everything and go that little bit further. And maybe that's why she was always so relieved to go away: because there she was Eloise Ashby, the woman who could make a difference and save the world. And although she never said anything to me—she would rather have died than admit it—I think she knew she wasn't that good at being a mum.'

'And for someone who wanted to be perfect,' Amy said softly, 'that would've been really tough to deal with. Maybe she wasn't rejecting you and Perdy, Tom. Maybe she felt that she was the one who couldn't live up to you, because—despite the fact you don't seem to realise it— you're a natural at parenting. And maybe she didn't let herself get close because she was terrified of failing and of Perdy rejecting her.'

'That never occurred to me,' Tom said, looking shocked. 'She was my wife. I loved her, Amy. I wouldn't have married her if I didn't.' He shook his head. 'If only she'd talked to me, told me how she felt.'

'When you think you have to be perfect, it's hard to admit weakness.'

Tom's eyes narrowed slightly. 'That sounds personal.'

'Not me—my parents. That's how they are. And that's OK: I understand that and I can accept them for what they are. That way, we get the best out of each other. I don't ask for things I know they can't give me, and they don't feel that they're letting me down.'

'How did you get to be so wise?' Tom asked, stroking her hair.

Because her best friend had helped her see it. Ex-best friend. Amy's throat tightened, and she evaded the question. 'I can tell you now, Perdy's really secure. I've heard you tell her you love her every single day.'

'Because I do. She's the light of my life.' He looked at

her. 'I can't ever remember Eloise's parents saying that to her. And, if yours were like hers, would I be right in guessing that they didn't say it to you?'

'It didn't occur to them,' she said dryly. 'And considering that my name means "beloved", that's pretty ironic. But Cassie and Joe did, when I was here. Every day they told their kids they loved them—and they always included me.'

'Do you see much of your parents?' he asked.

'Not really. We're on good terms, but we're just not that close. They're in the States right now.'

'You didn't think about taking your sabbatical there, spending time with them? Talking to them about what happened?' Tom asked.

Amy gave a dry laugh. 'It's not the kind of thing they'd be helpful with.'

'And Cassie and Joe aren't here.' He frowned. 'Did you talk to them before you left London?'

She shook her head. 'They were about to go and see Beth, ready to meet their first grandchild when he arrived. And now Sam's here I'm not going to rain on their parade. I want them to enjoy their first memories of their grandson, not have everything bogged down by me being a misery-guts.'

'So why don't you talk to me?'

Her breath caught. 'Talk to you?'

'Let me do for you what you just did for me. Same deal: I'll listen without judging.'

Talk about it.

Her heart rate sped up.

Could she?

'You've got surgery this morning,' she prevaricated.

He glanced at his watch. 'In an hour. Which means I've got fifty minutes. That's enough to make a start, at least.' His eyes held hers. 'Talk to me, Amy.'

CHAPTER EIGHT

Amy's skin suddenly felt too tight.

Talk about it.

No. She'd resisted the idea of counselling for a good reason. 'Talking won't change a thing.'

'Funny, someone told me not so long ago that it would make a difference. That talking won't change the past, but it might change the way you see things and help you deal with them.' He stroked her face. 'I didn't believe her—but guess what? She was right. I'm still angry and I still resent Eloise and her parents, but I can see my way to dealing with that now. I understand why I feel the way I do, and that's half the battle.'

She understood exactly why she felt the way she did. She didn't need to talk about it.

'Amy,' he said softly. 'Talk to me.'

She dragged in a breath. 'You might not want to know me when I tell you.'

He kept his arms round her. 'What's so bad? You lost a patient? Amy, you can't save everyone, and you know it. Just as I know that I can refer one of my patients to the top specialist in the country, but it still doesn't give a hundred per cent guarantee that the treatment will work.'

'I didn't lose a patient.' She frowned. 'Why would you think that?'

'You told Perdy you'd stopped being good at your job. I assumed it was an op that didn't go to plan.'

'You're right there.' She felt her mouth compress into a thin line. 'Except my patient didn't die.'

'What happened, then?'

'He survived. And he's been in constant pain ever since.' She swallowed hard. 'I'm supposed to be a pain specialist, and I screwed up.'

'You're human, Amy. Everyone makes mistakes.' He paused. 'Though I'd guess that you're always hard on yourself, so be honest with me—could anyone else have fixed it?'

'Maybe.'

'And maybe not,' he prompted. 'What happened?'

'It was a horse-riding accident. He was thrown and landed badly. And then the horse rolled on him.'

'So he had spinal cord damage?' Tom guessed.

She nodded. 'On the cusp. We weren't sure if it was C8 or T1.' Spinal injuries were referred to by the letter of the area of the spinal cord—cervical, thoracic, lumbar and sacral—and their position counting downwards from the top. Nerve damage above the first thoracic nerve, T1, meant that as well as paralysis in the legs, the arms would be paralysed and the muscles in the chest and abdomen would be affected, which in turn affected breathing and the ability to cough and clear the chest.

'He's going to be in a wheelchair for the rest of his life, dependent on everyone round him. He's never, ever going to be free of pain. And his career's gone down the tubes—you can't be a champion show-jumper if you can't even get into the saddle.'

'So he's suing you?'

'I'd feel better if he did.' She swallowed hard. 'But nothing I can do will ever make things better. Ever.'

'When did it happen?' he asked softly.

'Last October,' she said.

'But there's more to it than that.' It was a statement rather than a question.

She nodded. 'I'm not used to failing, Tom. I was a good surgeon. The fact I messed it up really knocked my confidence. And a couple of weeks ago I actually froze in an op. My head went completely blank. It was a textbook case and I couldn't remember what to do. All my training felt as if it had vanished from my head. There was nothing there any more: just a big, black hole.' She blew out a breath. 'Luckily I had one of the most talented juniors with me and he sorted it out. But it was beyond his training level, and if anything had gone wrong it would've been my fault. I was the lead surgeon; I was responsible. In charge.' She swallowed hard. 'I screwed up. So I did the right thing: I resigned.'

'So you're not actually on sabbatical?'

'Amazingly, I am. Though I don't deserve to be.' She blew out a breath. 'Fergus Keating—my boss—refused to accept my resignation. He told me to go away for three months and think about things.'

'Doesn't that tell you how much he values you? That you're too good at what you do for him to want to lose you?'

She sighed. 'I used to be good. But I've lost it, Tom. I can't do it any more.'

'Your confidence has completely gone because of one op that didn't go to plan, and which probably nobody else could've pulled off either,' Tom said thoughtfully. 'Why would a case get to you so much? Were you involved with him?'

'Not in the way you're thinking. But, yes, that's what Fergus said. It's why doctors are advised not to treat a relative or friend, because your emotions are involved and you don't see things clearly. In neurosurgery, there isn't room for mistakes. The structures are so delicate—the slightest wrong move can have catastrophic consequences. I deserve to be struck off for what I did.'

He frowned. 'I'm not following you, Amy. Your friend was in an accident, he damaged his spinal cord in a really critical place, you tried to help him, you just couldn't fix it. Perhaps I should admit that I looked you up on the internet.'

'You did what?' She stared at him, uncomprehending.

'I was curious. And I know it was wrong and I shouldn't have snooped. But, from what I've read about you,' he said softly, 'you're gifted. If you couldn't fix it, I'm damn sure nobody else could. You didn't do anything wrong and I bet you gave him more movement back than other people could've done. Does he have full finger movement?'

'I don't know.' The only people who could tell her that were Ben and Laura—and they weren't talking to her. Ever.

'If he does, he has you to thank. How can you be struck off for doing the best you possibly could?'

'Because I failed, Tom. I let Ben down.' Her throat hurt, and she swallowed. 'Worse, I let Laura down.'

'Laura?' he asked softly.

'His wife.' She could feel the tears welling up, the loss and misery rising to drown her again. 'My best friend,' she whispered. 'My best friend for the last sixteen years, and I've lost her.' She shuddered, willing the tears to stay back, but one spilled over anyway. Silently.

Tom said nothing, simply wiped it away with his thumb, and the sheer tenderness of the gesture almost undid her.

Now she'd started talking, the words kept spilling out.

'We met on the first day at university. I'd just unpacked my stuff and I was homesick as hell, and I went into the kitchen and she was there, making coffee. She made me a mug and shared her chocolate biscuits with me—her parents had sneakily repacked her case and added all sorts of treats.'

It was the sort of thing his parents had done, Tom remembered. And he'd guess that Amy's parents had been far too busy to think of a teenager taking her first steps out into the world and how to make it easier for her.

'It didn't matter that she was reading geography and I was a medic. We liked each other straight away. We liked the same kind of music, the same kind of films, the same kind of books. She was the best friend I'd ever had. Like a sister to me, as close as Beth was. I loved her so much, Tom. And I let her down. She trusted me to make Ben whole again, and I couldn't do it.'

She choked back a sob. 'Ben blames me for the fact he's a paraplegic, and so does Laura. She hasn't spoken to me since it happened. It's the first year since I've known her that she hasn't sent me a birthday card or a Christmas card.' Her teeth chattered. 'Laura made me a cake for my twenty-first birthday. In secret—I had no idea, though we shared a house. She even iced it. She's the only one apart from Cassie who's ever done anything like that for me. I love her so much and she's going through hell, and I can't support her through it because I'm the one who's caused her all the pain.'

'Amy, you did your best and nobody could ask more. Right now Laura's life has been turned upside down. She's hurting, and when you're in pain you lash out at those you love most—because they're safe to lash out at,' Tom said softly.

'She never, ever wants to see me again. I've tried calling

her, even writing her letters to tell her how sorry I am, but she can't forgive me, Tom. And I can't forgive me either.'

'Could anyone else have done the op?' he asked.

'We were the nearest hospital.'

'And you were the most senior neurosurgeon on duty?'

'It was me or nobody. Fergus was in Venice, celebrating his silver anniversary, and Luke, the other consultant, was off with the flu. I was the only one at the London Victoria who could do it. And if we'd sent him to a different hospital, further away, the nerve damage might've deteriorated to other vertebrae and he might've ended up losing his wrist and elbow flexion.'

'So, actually, you made the best of an impossible situation. You made the best decisions that could be made at the time.'

'It doesn't change the fact that I couldn't help him. That I let them down. Nothing's going to change that, Tom. Nothing's going to bring Ben's mobility back. And nothing's going to heal the rift between my best friend and me. I hate the fact I've lost her. But even more I hate myself for not being able to help her through this, to support her the way that she...' Amy dragged in a breath 'The way that she supported me when Colin broke up with me.'

She pulled away slightly, and he let her go.

'So now you know.'

He remembered what she'd said earlier: you might not want to know me when I tell you.

That could've gone for him, too. He'd never talked about how he felt about Eloise, because he hadn't wanted people to be disgusted by his selfishness. And yet he'd felt safe telling Amy: and he wanted her to feel safe, too. 'Thank you for telling me. And I'll keep your confidence.' He leaned forward and stole a kiss. 'I have a piece of information for you, Amy.'

'Information?'

'Uh-huh.' He held her gaze. 'I still want to know you.'

Tears filled her eyes again, but she blinked them back. 'Really?' Her voice was husky with pain.

'Really,' he confirmed. 'What you told me doesn't change my opinion of you at all.'

She swallowed hard. 'You'd better go. You'll be late for work.'

'I don't want to leave you right now.'

She shook her head. 'I'll be fine. You have patients who need you.'

True, but she needed him as well. Even if she wasn't going to admit it. He stroked her face. 'I do have patients, yes, but you're not fine.'

'I'll manage.'

'I know. You're strong. You're an amazing woman.' He held her close. 'I'll be back by one. And, just so you know, you and I are going to the beach just down the road. We're going to walk on the beach, hand in hand, have a paddle, and then we're going to have a picnic lunch.'

She frowned. 'Won't you have paperwork?'

He shrugged. 'I can sort that later, on my laptop. But you and I just went through the wringer again, relived some pretty dark stuff. I think we deserve to play hooky and get some fresh air, to make ourselves feel slightly more normal again—don't you?'

'Yes. Thank you. For listening and not judging.' She leaned forward slightly, resting against him.

'And thank you for doing the same.' He paused. 'I think we might be good for each other, Amy. In more than one way.' He gave her a last kiss. 'I'll see you at one, OK?'

'OK. Have a good morning.'

* * *

Tom's last patient that morning was the infamous Betty Jacklin. This time she was convinced that she had heart failure. 'I checked my symptoms against the book, and I've got them all. I've got dyspnoea, orthopnoea, cardiac asthma, nocturnal cough, fatigue, poor exercise tolerance, cold peripheries, and my muscles are wasting. So I've got left ventricular failure.'

There was one symptom she was missing, he noticed. Weight loss. And he could see no signs of cyanosis. He was pretty sure that his patient didn't have heart failure, but the fact that she kept coming back to the surgery with different symptoms told him that she was truly anxious about something. The different suspected medical conditions were a blind for the real problem, he was sure. Especially as she'd used medical terms rather than layman's. He'd just bet she had a medical textbook at home.

'Those are certainly the symptoms of LVF,' he said gently, 'but they're also symptoms of other diseases. I'd like to listen to your chest, if I may, and do a couple of tests. Is that all right?'

She went pink. 'Yes, Doctor.'

He listened to her chest. If she'd learned the symptoms off by heart, then he could reassure her bit by bit. 'The good news is, I can't hear a murmur.'

'What about wheezing?'

'There is a little, yes, but we'll talk about that when I've given you a breathing test and checked a couple of other things—because lots of things cause wheezing. I can't hear any crackles, so that's good. May I check your blood pressure?'

'Yes, Doctor.'

He did so. 'It's a hundred and thirty-five over eighty.'

'That's too high. It should be a hundred and twenty.' Her eyes widened.

'The bottom figure's the important one,' he said, 'because that's your blood pressure as your heart relaxes between beats. And you probably know from your reading that the top figure tends to rise as you get older because your arteries aren't quite as elastic as they are when you're young. But this is in line with your past readings, so I'm happy with it.'

She lifted her chin. 'You think I'm wasting your time, don't you?'

'No,' he said. 'I think you're worried, and I want to check you over. I also think,' he added gently, 'that reading medical textbooks is incredibly bad for you. It makes you worry yourself sick, literally. Can I tell you a secret?'

She went even pinker. 'Yes, of course, Dr Ashby.'

'Every medical student I know goes through exactly the same thing. They study the disease and its symptoms, and then start thinking how many symptoms they have. I convinced myself I had malaria once—and that was despite never having visited an area where there was malaria.'

She looked away. 'So you think I'm just being a silly old woman.'

'No,' he said again, 'you're worried, and I want to reassure you. I'd like to give you an ECG—I'm sure you know that that's a readout of the electrical activity of your heart—so I can see how your heart is beating.' He knew that they had an ECG machine at the surgery. 'Would you like to come with me, Miss Jacklin? It won't take very long.'

He talked her through what he was doing and why, acting on a hunch that she'd enjoy the medical terminology. And then he looked at the reading. 'It's absolutely fine,' he said, and talked her through the readings.

'So my heart isn't going too fast?'

'No, but when you're worried your heart rate tends to speed up,' he said. 'So I believe you absolutely when you said that your heart rate was too fast this morning.'

'And I do cough all the time.' She coughed then and there, as if to prove it.

'Can I get you to breathe into this tube for me?' he asked, taking out a peak flow meter. 'What I want you to do is to take a deep breath, and then blow out as hard as you can through this tube.'

She did so, and handed the tube back to him.

'For your age and height,' he said, 'you should be able to produce more. Given that you have a cough and you're wheezing... Do you have any tightness in your chest?'

'Well, yes. Sometimes.'

'Does anyone in your family have asthma, hay fever or eczema—or any other allergies?'

Miss Jacklin frowned. 'I had eczema when I was small. You think I have asthma?'

'With the symptoms you're describing, yes. Sometimes adults develop it.'

'Even at my age?'

'Or older than you,' he said, 'and it tends to go hand in hand with eczema and hay fever. I can give you an inhaler which will help stop you coughing and make breathing easier. You'll need two types—the reliever inhaler, which you use when you're having symptoms, and the preventer inhaler, which you use every single day.' He showed her how to use the inhalers. 'I'm going to want you to keep a diary for me over the next week to ten days, so I know when you've used your inhaler and when you've had symptoms. That will help me find the right dose for you to control the asthma.'

'So it's asthma?'

'I'm pretty sure it is,' Tom said, 'given what you've told me. You're right, the symptoms are similar to other conditions and that can make asthma hard to diagnose in adults—but the good news is that the other tests I did ruled out a heart condition. We have a special asthma clinic here, so you can make an appointment and see the nurse any time you're worried.'

She nodded. 'Thank you.'

'And, forgive me for being rude, you do need to lose some weight. That will help with the other symptoms you told me about.'

'My feet were really swollen this morning. I could hardly get my shoes on,' she said.

'It's been hot and humid lately,' he said gently, 'and lots of other people find the same thing in these weather conditions. Especially if they need to lose a bit of weight. Can I ask what your exercise routine is?'

'I don't have one. I told you, I have poor exercise tolerance. I get too breathless.'

'Part of that's because you're unfit, and the breathlessness is because of your asthma,' he said. 'Asthma can be brought on by exercise, and I'm not for a moment suggesting that you should take up running, but what I'd like you to do is start walking gently. Ten minutes, three times a day. If you've got a neighbour who has a dog, ask if you can go along for the walk. Or if there's a "walking for health" scheme here, try that—it's a great way of getting fresh air and making new friends.' He smiled at her. 'It'll be tough, the first few times, but you'd be surprised at how quickly it starts to make you feel better. The fitter you are, the better your heart works and the better your lungs work. It'll help your breathing, bring your heart rate down, get your muscles working and help you lose weight.'

'I see. Well, I'm sorry I wasted your time, Doctor.'

She looked almost about to cry. 'Miss Jacklin, you haven't wasted my time,' he reassured her. 'You're worried about your health, and that's what I'm here for—to listen to you, check your symptoms and see what's going on.'

'I bet you've got it written on my notes—that I'm always here and I'm a nuisance.'

'Nothing of the kind,' he said, 'and you're welcome to see for yourself.' He indicated the screen. 'But if you do come here a lot, my guess is that you're not telling us what you're really worried about and you're hoping we'll notice.' He smiled at her. 'I'm a good listener.' Amy had shown him that, earlier. 'Try me.'

She bit her lip. 'It's just... I was the one who never got married, so I looked after my mum. And since she died, the year before last, I've been on my own. My brothers have got their own lives—there's no room for me. I don't make friends easily. And I get so lonely.'

Mmm. He knew a little girl like that. And a woman who'd helped make it better. A woman who believed that what goes around comes around. Tom reached over to squeeze her hand. 'So you come here?'

She nodded. 'I know it's wrong and I know everyone laughs at me and thinks I'm a silly old woman, panicking over nothing.'

'Miss Jacklin, I'm not laughing at you,' Tom said. 'Loneliness is a horrible thing. And if you've been a carer for so long...it's hard when you stop being needed.'

She gulped. 'I miss her. I know she was bit of a curmudgeon, but I miss her.'

'Of course you do.' Tom looked at her. 'Did you have any bereavement counselling when she died?'

'No.'

'Some people find it helps. I can refer you, if you'd like me to.'

She shook her head. 'I've already taken enough of your time.'

He'd diagnosed her physical illness, but he still needed to deal with the emotional gap—the thing that kept Betty Jacklin reading her medical textbook and seeing symptoms in herself. And he had a feeling that he knew what could help her fill that gap. 'Did you used to read to your mum?' Tom asked.

'Yes—she couldn't see the telly very well, so it annoyed her. I used to read to her all the time.'

'Did you enjoy it?'

She nodded.

'Forgive me for being pushy, but have you thought about offering your services to the local nursing home? I bet there are residents there who are just like your mum—they can't see well enough to read for themselves and would love to have someone reading to them so they can enjoy books again,' Tom suggested. 'And you'd get to meet people that way, too.'

'They'd laugh at me.'

'Absolutely not. I think they'd be delighted and they'd take you up on the offer like a shot—and you'd be making a real difference to people's lives. Would you like me to make some enquiries for you?'

She shook her head. 'You're busy, Doctor.'

'I'm here,' he said, 'to help my patients. Which includes you.'

A tear brimmed over. 'That's so kind…'

'What goes around comes around,' Tom said gently, quoting Amy's favourite phrase. Amy had shown him kindness that morning. It was his turn to pass it on. And he knew that there would still be enough left for him to support Amy the way she'd supported him.

* * *

When Tom returned to Marsh End House—more than ten minutes late—Amy's eyes were still red and swollen, and he knew she'd spent the morning crying. It was something she'd really needed to do; he had the feeling that she'd locked all her grief and misery inside until today.

He wrapped his arms round her and they stood there, just holding each other.

'Sorry I'm late,' he said.

'Joe's surgeries always overrun,' she said. 'Cassie said you should never set your watch by a good GP, because they always put their patients first instead of thinking of beating the time targets.'

'That was a compliment—I think.' He smiled at her. 'Give me two minutes to change into something more suitable for the beach, and we'll go.'

'Sure.' She gave him a tentative smile. 'So did you have a good morning?'

'Great,' he said. 'You know those days when you think you might just have made a breakthrough?'

She swallowed hard. 'I used to.'

'And you will again,' he reassured her. 'I had one of those today. And it's thanks to you.'

She frowned. 'How do you work that one out?'

'Because you listened to me. And you reminded me how important it is to listen. I listened to one of my patients, today, so I worked out what she wasn't telling me.'

'What the real problem was, you mean,' she said.

'Absolutely. And I think I might have a solution, too. I need to pick your brains about that, later.'

She looked wary. 'Is this to do with neurology?'

'No, it's to do with the local area. Which you know better than I do. Nursing homes.'

'Nursing homes?' she echoed, sounding completely at a loss.

'Tell you in a minute.' Tom ran upstairs, dragged his suit off, changed into jeans and a T-shirt, and ran back downstairs.

Buster wagged his tail hopefully when Tom reappeared in the kitchen, and Tom made a fuss of him. 'Later. Promise,' he said, and Buster curled up in his bed, propped his chin on his paws and looked mournfully at him.

'I keep my promises and you know it, so don't you try and tell me you're a poor, sad, hard-done-by dog,' Tom said with a grin.

He shepherded Amy out to his car and drove them slightly further down the coast.

'So what's this about nursing homes?'

'I just wondered where they were. I haven't done any calls to one yet. I know someone who's a little bit lonely, and I think if she does some voluntary work—reading to elderly people who love books but it's too tough on their eyesight—it'll do wonders for her self-esteem, and it'll get her out of the house and give her an interest in life.'

'That's your breakthrough?'

'Yup. Can't say any more—patient confidentiality—but I hope everyone in the village will give her a chance. And it's a shame nobody picked up the root of the problem before.'

'Sometimes it's hard to see what's right in front of your nose,' Amy said.

He reached across to squeeze her hand. 'I'll remind you that you said that later. And you're right. It's easy to take things for granted.'

The beach was practically deserted—there were only a couple of dog-walkers—and they both took their shoes off and rolled up jeans and walked on the shoreline, hand in hand. The sea was incredibly calm, the waves lapping gently over their feet. 'This is like that music you were playing the other night,' he said.

'This coastline is my favourite place in the world, and that music reminds me of it,' she explained.

They walked until Tom's stomach rumbled. 'Ah. I have a confession. I forgot about the picnic,' he said.

'So did I,' Amy said.

'Never mind. We can get something from the shop on the harbour.'

'Crab sandwiches,' Amy said. 'Cromer crabs are the best in the world. And you can't be on this part of the coast and not try them.'

The kiosk at the harbour furnished them with crab salad wraps and chilled sparkling water; they leaned on the bonnet of Tom's car and watched the ships in the harbour as they ate.

'Seal trips,' Tom said, nodding at the sign. 'Have you ever been on one?'

'Years ago—I was probably about twelve,' Amy said. 'Perdy'd love it.'

'Then we'll go, one weekend,' Tom said. He paused. 'Amy, I'm not going to put any pressure on you. I'm the worst person in the world you could fall for—a single father who's struggling to do the right thing. I have no idea where this is going, and I know that neither of us is in a position to promise each other for ever. But I do think we can make each other feel better, for as long as we're both here.'

'And it's just between you and me,' Amy said. 'Not that you're my dirty little secret or I'm yours—just that it's easier that way. It avoids all the gossip and it'll make sure Perdy doesn't get hurt.'

'Deal.' Tom kissed her, very slowly. 'Though there's something I need to get on the way home.'

'Something?'

'Supplies,' he said, and enjoyed watching the colour rise in her face when she realised what he meant.

He left her in the car while he went to the supermarket, and returned carrying a huge bar of chocolate, which he dropped on her lap.

'Chocolate?' She blinked, looking surprised.

He grinned. 'I needed something to put on top of a certain box at the checkout.'

She grinned back. 'Anyone would think we were teen-agers.'

'Instead of being about to hit our mid-thirties and the quick slide to our forties,' he teased.

'Way over the hill,' she teased back.

He stole a kiss. 'Well, I happen to know the secret of youth.'

'Oh, yes?'

He kissed her again. 'I'll show you. But not until a lot later this evening. Or maybe tomorrow afternoon.'

She stroked his face and smiled. 'Consider that a date, Dr Ashby.'

CHAPTER NINE

It turned out to be the following afternoon. Tom managed to clear his mind and concentrate on his patients for morning surgery, but as soon as he set off for Marsh End House—back to Amy—he felt as if his blood was slowly heating in his veins.

And, weirdly, he was nervous.

This was mad, because they'd agreed to have an affair. A no-strings affair where neither of them was going to get hurt. This was completely mutual. A joint decision. He knew they both wanted this.

And yet he felt like a teenager on his first date.

How long had it been since he'd felt like this?

How long since he'd felt that heady anticipation of seeing a certain someone smile at him, and knowing that soon those lips would be teasing his? How long since he'd really looked forward to seeing someone simply because he enjoyed her company? How long since he'd trusted anyone enough to really talk to them, the way he'd talked to Amy?

He dropped his bag in the hallway then went in search of Amy. He'd half-expected to find her in the kitchen, or reading in the conservatory, but when Buster came bounding in from the garden it gave him a clue. He found her at the bottom of the garden, weeding Cassie's herbs.

'Hey.' He crouched down so that he was on her level, and eyed the pile in the wheelbarrow. 'Looks as if you've been busy.'

'I have. And I've discovered that I actually like gardening.' She smiled at him. 'When I get back to London, I might just invest in some pots for my patio and grow a few things.'

When I get back to London.

Of course he knew that she was going back at some point in the future. She'd never pretended otherwise. But it was a reminder: don't get attached. Don't let himself fall for her.

'Had a good morning?' she asked.

'Yes.' This was supposed to be the easy bit. Where he kissed her hello, she kissed him back, and he led her upstairs so he could kiss her exactly where he wanted to kiss her without fears of being overlooked or interrupted.

'Tom, are you OK?' she asked, looking concerned.

'Yes.' He smiled ruefully. 'No. I'm not used to this, Amy. I feel like a teenager, awkward as hell and I don't have a clue what I'm doing.'

She removed her gloves. 'If it helps, it's the same for me.'

'I got together with Eloise when I was nineteen. We'd known each other a year.' He shook his head in frustration. 'I can't even remember how you're supposed to act when you first…' He couldn't think how to phrase it without it sounding insulting.

'First start having an affair with someone?' she asked.

He nodded.

'Are are you sure you're ready for this?'

'Yes and no. I've been doing a lot of thinking. I'm not still in love with Eloise. If I'm honest about it, we'd been growing apart for months before she went away for the last time.' He sighed. 'I think that's part of the reason why I felt so guilty. I found it hard to mourn her because I'd already started getting used to the idea of her not being around.' He grimaced. 'Sorry, that makes me sound hard.'

'No, you're being honest.'

'What about you? Are you ready for this?'

'I'm not still in love with Colin, if that's what you're asking.'

'But you haven't got involved with anyone else since.'

'I was too busy at work.'

He arched an eyebrow at her.

She gave him a rueful smile. 'OK. So I used work to fill the gap. And then it became a habit, I guess. It was easier to concentrate on my work than take a risk on a relationship.' And now work had left a hole in her life. 'But I'm not using you to fill the gap left by work, if that's what you're thinking.'

'I know you're not. The same as I'm not using you to fill the gap in my life.' He paused. 'The first time between you and me—we didn't plan it. It took us both by surprise. That's why it felt as if I'd been unfaithful to her. But this time it's going to be different.'

She smiled at him. 'Tom Ashby, are you telling me that you're planning to seduce me?'

The teasing note in her voice gave him confidence. 'I seem to remember we have a date, Amy Rivers—even though I'm not actually taking you anywhere.'

She grinned. 'At least you're sparing me cheesy lines about taking me to paradise.'

He gave a hollow laughed. 'I'm out of practice and this is early days. Of course it's not going to be perfect. I haven't found out where you like being touched, where you like being kissed, what makes you go incoherent. But.'

Her eyes glittered with what he really, really hoped was desire. 'But?'

'I plan to,' he said, standing up. 'Starting now.'

She removed her gardening gloves and let him draw her to her feet.

And then he was kissing her under the trees at the bottom of the garden, with sunlight dappling through the leaves, birdsong filling the air, and the scent of blooming honeysuckle everywhere. He knew then he'd always associate those sounds and scents with Amy.

They walked indoors, holding hands, and he led her to his room.

Then he closed the door, drew the curtains, and turned to look at her, suddenly feeling out of his depth.

She was smiling. 'You look fabulous in a suit, Dr Ashby—but I also know you look fabulous out of it.' Her smile broadened. 'And I want to enjoy taking your clothes off.'

That smile did crazy things to his insides. 'I'm in your hands,' he said softly.

'Good.' She slid his jacket from his shoulders then hung it over the back of his chair. Slowly, she undid the buckle of his belt and excitement licked through his veins. By the time she'd lowered the zipper of his trousers, he was finding it hard to breathe normally, anticipating the moment when she'd touch his bare skin.

He heeled off his shoes and stepped out of his trousers, prepared to leave them where they were on the floor—but Amy scooped them up, smoothed out the creases and hung them over his jacket.

'What's this, you're a neat freak?' he teased.

'Control freak. I can do untidy when it suits me,' she said with a grin.

She undid his tie, carefully smoothing the creases out, and he realised what she was doing.

Making him wait.

Teasing him.

So that when she eventually touched him, it would blow his mind.

'Slow and easy, hmm?' he asked.

'Yup.' She moistened her lower lip, and desire kicked low in his stomach.

And then—at last—she started unbuttoning his shirt. He shivered as she pushed the soft cotton aside and flattened her palms against his chest. 'Nice pecs, Dr Ashby.'

Her voice was that little bit lower and huskier, and he knew this was affecting her just the same way.

She slid his shirt from his shoulders, again smoothing out the material and hanging it over his chair.

And then she took the waistband of his soft jockey shorts and drew them downwards.

Really, really slowly. By the time he'd stepped out of them and got rid of his socks, he was quivering, his whole body yearning for her to touch him more intimately.

'Do you have any idea what you've done to me?' he asked hoarsely.

She curled her fingers round his erection and looked very pleased with herself. 'Exactly what I planned to do.'

'What's sauce for the goose...' He took the hem of her T-shirt between thumb and forefinger and slowly lifted it up. She lifted her hands above her head, letting him take off the T-shirt—and he dropped it on the floor.

'Hey, now that's not fair—I left your clothes neat and tidy,' she protested.

He grinned. 'I'm less patient than you are.' He traced a forefinger along the lacy edges of her bra. 'You feel good,

Amy. So soft. I want to touch you. Taste you.' He un-snapped her bra and let her breasts spill into his hands, teasing her hardening nipples with his thumbs. 'Gorgeous. You've filled out a bit.'

She raised an eyebrow. 'Are you saying I'm fat?'

'No, I'm saying you were too thin when I first met you, but a month here has changed you.' He traced the curve of her cheekbones with the tip of his forefinger. 'You've lost some of the shadows under your eyes.'

'I'm sleeping better now. Not so many bad dreams,' she admitted. 'And talking to you about all the stuff I'd kept inside…it's helped. A lot.'

'Good. You helped me, too.' He let his hands slide down her body to her waist, and undid her jeans, pushing the faded denim down over her hips. 'You're all curves, your skin's so soft, and I find it really difficult to keep my hands off you—oh, and have I told you that your mouth is really, really sexy?'

'No, but I'm glad to hear it.' She rubbed the pad of her thumb along his lower lip. 'So's yours.'

He caught her thumb between his lips, drew it into his mouth and sucked, delighted when her pupils darkened.

'I'll tell you something else that's sexy,' she said. 'Your glasses.'

'My glasses?' He blinked. 'How?'

'They make you look like a geek.'

He raised an eyebrow. 'A geek? I thought geeks had no social skills?'

'No, that's a nerd,' Amy corrected him. 'Geeky is the new sexy. Clever men are hot.'

'And you're telling me because…?'

'Oh, that's the most outrageous fishing for a compliment I've ever heard.' She laughed. 'All right, Dr Ashby. You're clever—and you're hot. Especially in those glasses.'

He laughed back. 'Well, I'm afraid I need to take them off—because they're going to get in the way of what I want to do to you.'

'Sounds interesting.'

'It will be.'

'Let me,' she said, gently lifting the frames from his face; she placed them carefully on his bedside cabinet.

Tom cupped her face between his hands and kissed her, gently at first and then more fiercely as she opened her mouth beneath his, letting him deepen the kiss.

It was the work of seconds to finish removing the rest of her clothes; then he pushed his duvet aside, picked her up and dropped her on the bed.

'What was that for?' she asked, laughing up at him.

'Just to let you know that I have a Neanderthal side.'

'I'd noticed. What happened to slow and easy?'

'A little variation's a good thing. But if you want me to take it slowly...' He stooped to kiss her lightly, and then kissed his way down her body, noting what made her wriggle and push herself against him, and what drew little murmurs of delight from her. He took his time, covering every centimetre of skin, from the hollows of her collar-bones down to the soft underside of her breasts, her hipbones and her navel.

When she parted her legs in silent assent, inviting him to touch her more intimately, he retreated to the foot of the bed.

She opened her eyes. 'Tom?'

'Slowly, you said.' He kissed the hollow of her ankle, and she quivered.

'You're teasing me,' she protested.

'No. I'm seducing you, Amy,' he corrected softly, and took a slow, gentle path up to the backs of her knees. By the time he'd reached her inner thighs, she was clearly having trouble concentrating. And the first glide of his finger down her sex had her arching almost off the bed.

He pushed one finger inside her, and she whimpered.

When he touched the tip of his tongue to her clitoris, she slid her hands into his hair. 'Tom, I can't hold on much longer.'

That was the whole idea, he thought with an inward grin. He wanted her to lose control with him. Completely.

He teased her with his mouth and his fingers until he felt her tense, and then he felt her shudder and her body tightening around him. When the little aftershocks of her climax had died down, he shifted up the bed next to her. 'Better?'

'Uh. Yes. Thank you,' she whispered.

'Good. Because I don't think I can do slow right now,' he said. 'I want you *now*, Amy.'

Her mouth opened in a little sigh of assent and pleasure, and he rummaged in the drawer for the box of condoms. He opened the packet, his hands shaking slightly; and then at last he was kneeling between her thighs. Right where he wanted to be.

She reached up to touch his face, encouraging him, and he fitted the tip of his penis to her entrance.

'Tom,' she whispered, and he was lost. He eased into her, pushing deep, and she shuddered. 'Tom, yes.'

She met him kiss for kiss, thrust for thrust. As she arched up against him, tipping her head back, he took the opportunity to kiss her throat. He could feel her pulse thudding hard against his tongue; clearly he was having the same effect on her as she was on him. Needed this. Wanted this.

He pushed deeper, and she wrapped her legs round his waist, pulling him closer.

Time felt as if it were splintering, and then he was falling,

falling—and taking her with him, because he heard her cry out his name at the exact moment that his climax hit.

When he'd dealt with the condom, he came back to bed, drawing her into his arms so her head rested against his shoulder. Neither of them spoke, but the silence was comfortable. Drowsy. He would've liked to fall asleep in her arms, but it wasn't an option—not with the school run due. He sneaked a glance over the top of her head at his clock. Good. They didn't have to move yet.

He stroked her hair. 'I love your hair,' he said softly.

'You do?' She sounded surprised.

'Why wouldn't I?'

'I thought men were supposed to like long hair.'

Interesting. So had she chopped her hair because it had been long when she'd been engaged to Colin? Though the look in her eyes warned him not to ask. 'It makes you look cute. Like Tinkerbell.'

'Tinkerbell?' She blinked. 'So what does that make you? Peter Pan or Captain Hook?'

He kissed the tip of her nose. 'Amy Rivers, do I detect a pirate fantasy?'

She grinned. 'Maybe.'

'I can swagger and roll my Rs. The hat might be a problem, though.'

'Pity. But, just so you know, I was thinking Captain Sparrow rather than Captain Hook.'

He laughed. 'That's easily sorted. Lend me your eyeliner and imagine the hat.'

She laughed back. 'And you'd grow your hair long, would you?'

'You like men with long hair?' he asked, surprised. He'd expected her to go for someone in a sharp suit.

'My teenage crushes were all on rock stars,' she admitted.

He stole a kiss. 'Don't tell me you operated to rock.'

'I always played Corelli in Theatre. Because it's calming,' she said. 'But rock's good for hitting the treadmill afterwards.'

'So that's how a neurosurgeon relaxes? Hard exercise?'

'I play a mean game of squash, too.'

'I used to,' he said. 'I'm almost tempted to challenge you.'

'Oh, yes?'

He stole another kiss. 'There would be forfeits involved.'

'I think I like the way your mind works, Tom Ashby.'

'Yours, too.' And he did like her. This was more than a physical thing: he actually liked who Amy was. And he felt comfortable with her—more comfortable than he could remember feeling with anyone for a long, long time. He could talk to her about anything, and it was as if he'd known her for years instead of only a month. 'I'm sorry I pushed you into talking about neurosurgery the other day.'

'Honestly, it was fine. Actually, I enjoyed it,' she said. 'And it's made me think about it—made me realise how much I miss it.'

'Enough to go back to it?' he asked.

She shook her head. 'I can't trust myself. What happens if I lose it again in an op? Danny coped brilliantly, but I might not be so lucky with my junior next time. I can't risk my patients like that.'

He drew her closer and stole a kiss. 'And then again, there's the possibility that you won't lose it again. Because now you've started talking about it, dealing with the thing that made you freeze.'

'I can't trust myself, Tom,' she repeated.

'OK. Suppose you decide not to go back to neurosurgery. What options does that leave you?'

'I don't know.' She bit her lip. 'Maybe I should retrain for something completely different.'

'Would you be happy not being a doctor?'

She shrugged. 'I probably need to go and talk to a recruitment agency and do some tests to see what else I might be good at.'

No, Tom thought, you wouldn't be happy. You're a doctor and you were a good one; and you'd be a huge loss to the profession.

Though maybe he could do something about that. Perhaps he'd have a quiet word with Marty, the acting head of the practice. 'Maybe,' he said, 'your boss was right and you just need some time. Yesterday was the first time you'd talked about it—really talked—and it's still early days. Don't rush yourself.'

'Maybe.'

At least she hadn't rejected the idea out of hand. He stole a last kiss. 'Much as I'd love to spend the rest of the afternoon here with you, I need to be going,' he said.

'School run?'

He nodded.

She kissed him lingeringly. 'I'll let you have the shower first, then.'

'If I wasn't short on time,' he said, 'I'd suggest you sharing it with me. But I don't think my self-control's going to be good enough. So I'm going to be ungentlemanly and take you up on your offer. And next time we're going to hit the shower first and I can do what I have in mind.'

'Is that a promise?'

'You bet.'

On the Saturday, Perdy shyly asked Amy to go with her and Tom to see the seals. Amy loved seeing the little girl's eyes go big and round with wonder as they neared the spit of sand at Blakeney Point and saw the seals.

'Look,' Perdy said, taking her hand and pointing.

On the rocks, seals were basking in the sun. One rolled over and flapped a flipper.

'It's waving to us,' Perdy said, looking delighted. 'It's so cute! Look, Daddy, there's a family.'

The bull, large and protective; the cow, secure next to her mate; and the pup, settled happily and cuddled up to its parents.

Some of the seals, more inquisitive than the others, made their cumbersome way into the water, and then suddenly they were gliding along, their heads bobbing up and disappearing and bobbing up again an impossible distance away.

'Let me take a photo of you and your dad,' Amy said, taking her camera out of her bag. They were relaxed together, smiling; it was a wonderful picture and one she guessed that Tom's parents would love. Maybe it would help to soften Eloise's parents, too, seeing their granddaughter looking happy and loved. 'And if you want to take some pictures of the seals, Perdy, I'll print them out when we get home. Maybe you could take them in to show and tell at school next week.'

The middle-aged woman opposite them leaned forward. 'I know how it is when one of you is always behind the camera. Would you like me to take a photograph of the three of you?'

Amy wanted to say yes, but she knew she didn't really have any rights. While she was still dithering about what to say, Tom smiled. 'Thank you, that'd be really kind of you. We'd love a picture of the three of us.' Gently, he prised Amy's camera from her fingers and handed it to the woman.

'Get a bit closer—that's it, perfect.'

Amy's pulse started tattooing. This felt like being a family—Perdy cuddled between the two of them. Just as it had been with Colin and Millie.

And she hadn't learned a thing from all the heartbreak. So much for her promise to herself not to get involved.

Yet how could she have resisted?

'Thank you,' she said, hoping that her voice didn't sound as cracked as it felt.

'Your little girl looks so much like your husband,' the woman said as she handed the camera back.

'Yes, Perdy's the image of Tom.' The moment the words were out, she regretted them. What the hell had she been thinking? Perdy wasn't her little girl, any more than Millie had been. Of course she couldn't step into Eloise's place. Although Tom had said he was no longer in love with Eloise, he'd been faithful to her since they got together when he'd been nineteen. You couldn't just brush aside fifteen years of loving someone, even if you were deeply angry with them, and as for Perdy... Nobody could just elbow your mother aside, even if you hadn't been that close. Given that Tom had hinted how Eloise had struggled with parenthood, Amy guessed that Perdy had been like herself, desperate for her mother's approval and not sure whether she was really loved. But Perdy still hadn't talked about it to her, so Amy was relying entirely on a guess.

She didn't dare look at Tom or Perdy, unable to bear to see the censure in their eyes. But now she'd said it. She couldn't unsay it. And if she explained to the woman now, it would be awkward and embarrassing for all of them.

For a moment, she really wished they hadn't come on the seal trip.

She felt the pressure of Tom's fingers against her arm and forced herself to meet his gaze.

'You OK?' he mouthed.

Trust him to have picked up on her fears. Tom Ashby was a perceptive man. But she was used to being bright, sparkly, smiling Amy on the outside, covering for the confused and hurting Amy inside. She gave him the full megawatt treatment, mouthing back, 'Sure.'

Even if he did know she was lying, to her relief he didn't call her on it.

When they finally got home, Perdy hugged her tightly. 'It's been one of the best days of my life. Thank you so much.'

Amy found herself really hugging the little girl back, a lump in her throat. 'I loved it too,' she said, her voice cracked.

And not just the day.

She was really falling for Tom and his daughter.

'And what that lady said on the boat about you being my mum—that was wrong,' Perdy said.

Amy froze. Oh, no. She'd really hoped that the little girl hadn't picked up on that. 'I'm sorry,' she said softly.

'My mum wouldn't have gone to see the seals with me and Dad,' Perdy said. And all of a sudden her face crumpled. 'She didn't do things with me because she didn't love me. That's why she went away and died.'

Tom looked stricken; he dropped straight to his knees and wrapped his arms round his daughter, holding her tightly. 'Darling, it wasn't your fault your mum went away,' he told her fiercely. 'And of course she loved you.'

'She never said. Not like Alexis's mum does. She never came to see me in the Christmas play or on sports day. And she went away.'

'It was the just way your mum was, darling. She felt she

had to try harder than anyone else and be better than anyone else.'

'But I overheard Granny and Grandpa saying I was an accident.' Perdy's voice was shaky.

'I've always wanted you, Perdy, always,' he reassured her. 'Yes, you did come along a little bit earlier than we planned, but you were always wanted. The day we found out we were expecting you was one of the best of my life—and even better than that was the day you arrived. I held you when you were three minutes old and you were the most beautiful baby I'd ever seen. You still are. I love you, I'm very proud of you, and nothing will ever change that.'

Her breath hitched. 'But my mum didn't, did she?'

Amy could see on Tom's face that the question almost broke his heart. She dropped to her knees beside them and wrapped her arms round both of them. 'Perdy, I didn't know your mum, but she sounds a lot like mine,' she said softly. 'My mum never ever tells me that she loves me, or that she's proud of me. But that's just because some people aren't very good at telling people they love them. I used to think she didn't love me, but when I grew up I realised that she does really. She just doesn't say it because that's how she is. So I reckon your mum definitely loved you. Anyone would be proud to have a kind, sweet, lovely girl like you as a daughter.'

Tom sent her a look of gratitude above Perdy's head. 'Your mum loved you, Perdy,' he said. 'She always had a photograph of you in her purse.'

'So she didn't go away because she didn't love me?'

'No. She went away because she didn't love herself enough,' Tom said softly. 'Grown-ups can be complicated. She might not have said it the way she should have done, but she definitely loved you, darling. And so do I. Very, very much. Nothing's ever going to change that. You'll always be the most important person in my life.'

Later that evening, when Perdy was asleep, Tom collapsed on the sofa in the conservatory next to Amy.

'OK?' she asked.

'Yes.' He gave a mirthless laugh. 'No. I had no idea she felt like that. And I could throttle Eloise's parents for not being more careful. Why on earth would they say something like that in the first place? And then make it worse by not checking that she couldn't overhear them?'

'They're not used to having kids around,' Amy said.

'No wonder she never talked to me about Eloise. She thought it was all her fault. And I…'

Amy curled her hand round his. 'You said the right things—you told her what she needed to hear. And she knows how much she means to you, Tom.' She paused. 'So Eloise really did carry a picture of her?'

'Yes.' He looked grim. 'I used to sort out the school photos and make sure there was a wallet-sized one in her purse as well as in my own wallet.'

'Tom, don't hate her for it. You can't change the past,' Amy said softly. 'And at least you know now. It's out in the open and you can deal with it.'

'And you helped. What you said…'

'Perdy reminds me a lot of how I was as a child,' Amy said. 'She's dealing with some of the same things I had to deal with, so I can understand some of how she's feeling.'

'Thanks for taking her side.'

'Tom, of *course* I'd take her side. And I meant what I said. Any mother would be proud to have a daughter like her.'

'Yeah.' He drew her closer. 'In some ways I'm glad this

happened today and not yesterday, just before I rang
Eloise's parents. Or I might just have exploded down the
phone at them.'

'You're taking her to see them?'

'Against my better judgement, yes.' He sighed. 'We're
going to see them next Saturday morning and coming back
on Monday, as it's half-term.'

'Tom, I know you're angry with them—and you have
every right to be—but it's worth building those bridges. For
Perdy's sake, if nothing else.'

'Maybe. I've managed to get two days off, but I'm not
the only one in the practice who wants time off over half-
term.' He looked serious. 'Maybe I'll ask Alexis's mum if
Perdy can go round to play when I'm at the surgery, and
I'll take both girls out somewhere when I'm off.'

Even though Amy's head was telling her not to do it—
that she really couldn't afford to get any more involved—
she couldn't help offering. 'Tom, I'm around all day, and
I'm perfectly happy to keep an eye on Perdy.'

'Thanks for the offer, but I don't want to be unfair and
take all your time.'

'I don't mind taking the girls to the beach, poking round
rock pools and looking for pretty shells—I used to love
doing that at their age,' she said. 'And I'll have fun reliving
my own childhood.'

'Really? You're not just being nice?'

She couldn't help smiling. 'I'm not just being nice.
They're lovely kids and we'll have a lot of fun.'

'Then thank you. Your offer's very gratefully accepted.'

But she could still feel the tension in his body. 'What
aren't you telling me?'

'How do you know?'

'I just do.'

'Boundaries,' he said. 'I'm about to encroach on yours again.'

'Hit me with it,' she said dryly.

'You know my patient with trigeminal neuralgia? She's seen the neurologist, and I had a note from him to say that he's going to send her for the gamma knife stuff. So I was wondering... I know it's an imposition, but you know so much more about it than I do.'

'You want me to talk to her?'

'Would you?'

It wasn't an actual operation, so she couldn't mess it up. 'All right. I'll get one of the frames so she can see exactly what's involved and that it won't hurt. Give me a couple of days to get it organised—I could see her maybe Friday?'

'Thank you.' He kissed the tip of her nose. 'She'll appreciate it—and so do I.'

CHAPTER TEN

On Wednesday morning, Amy rang her boss; Della, Fergus's secretary, put her straight through.

'Amy, it's marvellous to hear you,' Fergus said warmly. 'How are you doing?'

'OK, thanks,' she said. 'And you were absolutely right. I needed time off to get my head together. How are you?'

'I'm fine. So what can I do for you?'

'I'm on the scrounge,' she said. 'Can I borrow a stereo-tactic head frame?'

'You want to borrow…?' Fergus sounded surprised. 'What, are you planning to set up a treatment centre some-where in Norfolk?'

She laughed. 'As if I could afford the kit! No, it's just to reassure someone who's being sent for treatment. One of Tom's patients.'

'Tom?'

'My uncle's locum. We're sharing the house-sitting and dog-sitting between us,' she explained. 'His patient's having gamma knife treatment for TGN and he wants me to run through it with her. I thought it'd help if she actually saw one of the frames, so she didn't worry that it was going to be incredibly heavy or she was going to have enormous holes in her head from the pins.'

'I'll courier one over,' Fergus said.

'And I'll courier it straight back,' she promised.

'That's my girl.' He paused. 'You sound a lot happier, Amy. I think this sabbatical is good for you. But, even if you feel ready to come back now, we're sticking to the rules. You're not coming back until the three months is up.'

'What is this, absence makes the heart grow fonder?' she teased.

He laughed. 'Something like that. We all miss you, Amy. But I want you back whole.'

'I think I've turned a corner,' she said. Thanks to Tom, she added mentally.

'So you're talking to someone?'

'Sort of.' Not quite in the way Fergus meant, but she was getting there.

'Good. Right, I'd better go and sweet-talk Della into sorting out a courier for me, then.'

'Thanks, Fergus. For everything,' she said softly.

On Friday morning, Amy went into the surgery with Tom, and was surprised at just how warmly everyone greeted her.

Marty, the acting senior partner in Joe's absence, came in to Tom's consulting room to see her before the patients arrived and shook her hand heartily. 'It's lovely to see you, Amy. Joe said you were coming to stay for a while and I hoped you'd drop in to see us.' He grinned at Tom. 'I remember this one when she was knee-high to a grasshopper. Every summer she'd come in and polish the skeleton in Joe's office. Fascinated with it, she was.'

Amy rolled her eyes. 'Yeah, yeah. And now you're going to tell the story of how I made you tell me the name of every single bone in Latin.'

Tom grinned. 'How old were you?'

'Old enough,' she said tartly.

'She was five,' Marty confided. 'A born doctor. How are you getting on with Joseph's casebooks, Amy?'

'They're fascinating. When I've sorted out the transcripts, I'll let you have a copy,' Amy promised.

'I'd love that. Thanks.' He paused. 'Amy, I know you're on sabbatical, but I was wondering if I could be a bit cheeky and persuade you to run a couple of pain-relief clinics while you're here? We have a few patients who suffer from chronic pain and I think they'd really benefit from your help.'

She glanced at Tom: was he behind the offer? But his expression was unreadable.

'I... Marty, you've caught me a bit on the hop. Can I be terribly rude and ask if you'd mind if I think about it and get back to you?'

'Not at all, my dear girl.' He patted her arm. 'I know I shouldn't be impinging on your time but when Tom said you were coming in to have a chat with Mrs Cooper about her treatment, I couldn't pass up the chance to have a word and...' He smiled. 'Well. We'd be very pleased to have you.'

She raised an eyebrow at Tom when Marty had left. 'Was that anything to do with you?'

Tom lifted his hands in the classic 'surrender' position. 'All I did was mention to Marty that you were coming in to see Mrs Cooper, and that listening to you talk about procedures was a revelation.'

'So doing a pain clinic was all Marty's idea?'

'I think it's a really good one. But it's entirely your decision.'

'I'll think about it,' she said.

It was time for Tom's first patient. Mrs Cooper came into the consulting room and Tom introduced her to Amy.

'It's so kind of you to have a word with me.'

'My pleasure. I believe Dr Ashby's already given you an idea of what's involved, so I've borrowed a stereotactic head frame from my department to give you a chance to have a look at it.' She took the frame from its protective box on Tom's desk and handed it over.

'It feels lighter than I thought it would be,' Mrs Cooper said, sounding surprised. 'And you really have to pin it to my head?'

'So it doesn't move, yes. Can I show you?' At Mrs Cooper's nod, Amy smiled. 'I'll put it on Dr Ashby rather than on you, because I know the lightest touch can set off the pain and I don't want to do that to you. Dr Ashby, would you mind moving round in your chair so I can stand behind you?'

'Of course, Dr Rivers.'

She didn't bother correcting him that it was 'Ms'; patients had enough to worry about without the niceties of etiquette.

She put the square section of the frame over his head, just about resisting the urge to stroke his hair. 'It takes about ten to fifteen minutes to put it all into place, but don't worry, the doctors will explain it all to you again before they do it. We'd put local anaesthetic in here, here, here and here…' she brushed Tom's hair back and placed the tip of her forefinger against his skin '…and then, when that's had a chance to work, we'll put in the pins to fix the frame in place. It's really important because it keeps your head still and lets us be really precise with the radiation, so we know it's going to the right spot. You'll be aware of it, but it's not heavy and it's not painful because of the anaesthetic.'

She noticed how anxious Mrs Cooper looked and guessed exactly what she was worried about: the same thing all her patients worried about. 'It sounds really scary, but all my patients have said that it's a lot less traumatic than they expected.' She removed the frame again and put it back in the box before resuming her place next to Tom.

'Are you going to shave my head?'

'Absolutely not,' Amy said with a smile.

'And the gamma knife thing—it's not going to hurt?'

'Not at all,' Amy reassured her, and ran through the procedure for her as she had for Tom, keeping her explanations clear and simple; Tom chipped in, here and there, and it struck Amy how good he was with his patients. He could read their moods accurately, guess what their fears were, and he was great at reassuring them.

'When you've had your MRI scan, your consultant will have an image of your trigeminal nerve, and will mark it up with the planned dose distribution. I can show you some examples, if you like.'

'Could you?'

She'd already powered up her laptop so all she had to do was lift the screen. 'This is one of the "slices" that an MRI scan takes. The narrow bit at the top is your face, and these bits at the side are your ears.' She pointed out the nerve on the screen. 'This is the nerve that causes all the pain. And this image to the right is the same one, but those green lines show us where we're going to concentrate the radiation—how many shots and in which area.'

'It's marvellous what they can do nowadays,' Mrs Cooper said, looking awed. 'And that's what you do in London?'

'Yes.'

'They're sending me to London for the op—the London Victoria.'

Amy's hospital: and the name gave her a real pang. 'Then you might even have this very headset, because that's where this one came from. My boss sent it down for me.'

'So will you be the one treating me?'

'Probably not,' she said gently, 'because I'm on sabbatical at the moment. But I do know all the staff there, and they're absolutely excellent.'

'If they're like you,' Mrs Cooper said, 'I know I'll be in good hands and I won't have to worry about a thing.'

Amy had to swallow the lump in her throat. 'Thank you. Is there anything you'd like to ask me?'

'I don't think so, not right now.'

'OK. But do let Dr Ashby know if there is.'

'Any time,' Tom added.

'And you can always ask at the hospital,' Amy said. 'If you're worried about anything, no matter how silly it is, just ask. Nobody minds—we'd all much rather have a relaxed patient than one who's worried sick and too scared to ask anything.'

'Thank you, Dr Rivers.'

Looking considerably less tense, Mrs Cooper left the consulting room, closing the door behind her.

'You were brilliant,' Tom said softly. 'You've really helped her.'

'I hope so.'

'If you'd been in London, would you have been the one operating?'

'Probably.' And it hit her how much she missed it. Talking to patients, reassuring them the way she'd just reassured Mrs Cooper, and then performing the delicate and complex operation that took away all the pain. 'She'll probably be with Luke or Fergus—the other consultant or the head of Neuro—so she'll be absolutely fine. They're both sweethearts and really good at their job.'

'I know someone else who's a sweetheart,' Tom said. 'And who's a lot better at her job than she thinks she is.'

Something of her discomfort must have shown in her

face, because he pulled her onto his lap and stole a kiss. 'All right. I'll shut up. But thanks for helping out, Amy. You've made a real difference.'

'Maybe.' How easy it would be to let herself relax against him. But she dared not. She wriggled off his lap and packed away her laptop and the frame. 'I'd better get this frame couriered back to Fergus. See you later.'

Amy spent the rest of the day wondering: should she do the pain clinic? It would be a way of easing herself back in to medicine. 'Then again,' she said to Buster, 'supposing I screw up again?'

The dog rested one paw on her knee so he could reach up and lick her face.

'You old softie,' she said, making a fuss of him.

But it filled her thoughts to the point where she didn't do much on Joseph's casebooks. And the house felt so quiet, with neither Tom nor Perdy there. She knew that Perdy had arranged to go to Alexis's after school and Tom was going to pick her up after he'd seen his last patient; and she was shocked to find herself clock-watching until she heard the front door open and Buster rushed out to greet them.

Amy followed at a more sedate pace, carrying an empty coffee mug as an excuse to head for the kitchen.

'Here she is.' Tom presented her with an armful of pink-and-white spray carnations.

'You bought Amy flowers?' Perdy's eyes widened.

'Not me. One of my patients,' Tom explained. 'Amy came and had a chat with her about an operation she's going to have, and she wanted to say thank you. Mrs Cooper asked me to give you these,' he added to Amy.

'That's very sweet of her,' Amy said. Of course Tom wasn't going to give her flowers. This thing between them was private. And it was ridiculous to feel disappointment sinking through her because the flowers were from someone else. 'I'll put them in water,' she said, forcing herself to sound brighter than she felt. 'I was thinking of making fajitas for dinner tonight, and a strawberry and rhubarb crumble. Want to help me, Perdy?'

'Can I?' Perdy beamed at her. 'I'll go and wash my hands.'

And the evening passed exactly as she remembered spending evenings here during her childhood: full of laughter and fun, split between the kitchen and the garden.

On Saturday morning, Tom and Perdy left for Cheshire; and by lunchtime everything felt flat.

'It's ridiculous that I should miss them,' Amy told Buster. 'This is temporary. I'm going back to London in six weeks—less than that, maybe.'

The dog simply wagged his tail.

In the early afternoon, Tom sent her a text to let her know they'd arrived safely. Amy suppressed disappointment that he hadn't added a personal message; but they'd made no promises, and it was unfair of her to expect him to treat her like his girlfriend. They'd agreed this was a temporary thing, and she had no right to ask him to change it.

She forced herself to concentrate on Joseph's casebooks then took the dog for a run. Cooking for herself felt like too much of a bother, so she made herself a cold chicken salad, and Buster ended up with most of the chicken.

Sunday was more of the same; and Amy was idly sorting through the digital photographs on her laptop when she came across the picture from the seal trip. Herself and Tom either side of Perdy, cuddled in close, all three of them smiling broadly.

They looked like a family.

The shock of realisation felt as if someone had dropped

her into a deep pool of icy water and it took her a moment to catch her breath. This was what she wanted. What she'd been missing ever since Colin had changed his mind.

But would Tom be prepared to take a risk on her and let her be a family with him and Perdy? And, if he was, could she be brave enough to take that risk? If he changed his mind, the way Colin had, she didn't think she'd be able to handle rejection a second time.

Just after lunchtime on Monday, Tom texted her again to let her know they were on their way back to Norfolk.

Pasta, salad and garlic bread for dinner—ready ten minutes after you get back, she texted back.

She knew the journey took almost five hours. Add in some time for stops, and they'd be home at about seven, she calculated. And from half past six she found herself watching the clock, listening out for the crunch of tyres on gravel.

At last, Buster woofed and bounded down the hall.

'Hey, what a welcome,' Tom said, making a fuss of the dog.

Perdy dropped to her knees and hugged him. 'I've missed you so much! Grandma only has a cat and it's like the Siamese cats in *Lady and the Tramp*—horrible!'

Amy hung back in the kitchen, pretending that she was concentrating on reheating the sauce and cooking the pasta, and feeling suddenly shy and awkward. They'd been apart for a couple of days. Would Tom have come to his senses and changed his mind about her? Would they be having a 'Dear Jane' conversation once Perdy was asleep?

But then Perdy raced into the kitchen and hugged her. 'I missed you, too, Amy.'

There was a huge lump in her throat and it was as much as she could do to say, 'And I missed you.' But she hugged the little girl back just as fiercely.

'I've got the kettle on. You must be desperate for a cup of tea,' she said as Tom walked in.

'Thanks, I am,' he said. And his eyes sent her another message, that he was desperate to hold her: and everything suddenly felt all right with Amy's world.

Once they'd eaten, Amy had tidied the kitchen and Perdy had gone to bed after negotiating extra reading time, Tom drew Amy into the conservatory. His kiss was slow and sweet and promising, and then he just held her for a while, resting his face against her shoulder.

'I missed you,' he said softly.

'I missed you, too,' Amy admitted. 'How was it?'

'Not as bad as I expected. We had quite a long talk, and I made very sure that Perdy was asleep before we covered the difficult stuff.' He swallowed hard. 'It turns out they feel responsible for Eloise's death, too. And they realise how many mistakes they made with her. Mistakes they're not going to make with Perdy: I think they're going to make more of an effort with her now. They're going to ring her more, take an interest in what she does, the way my parents do.'

'That's good, Tom. You were right to build that bridge.'

'I couldn't have done it without you getting me to look at things differently.' He kissed her again. 'Thank you.'

'Amy, will you come to the beach and make sandcastles with us?' Perdy asked the following morning.

Amy knew it would be safer for her own peace of mind to refuse. But how could she resist that shy smile, those gorgeous eyes that were so like Tom's? Knowing that she was setting herself up for heartbreak and not being able to stop herself, she said, 'I'd love to.'

Between the three of them, they'd built an elaborate castle with a moat, and Perdy and Amy were just about to go to fill their buckets with seawater for the moat when they heard a woman screaming, 'Help! Somebody, please help!'

Tom looked over in the direction of the screams; they could see a woman cradling a child. 'Looks like one for us,' he said.

Amy nodded, and the three of them sprinted over.

'We're both doctors,' Tom said. 'What's wrong?'

'It's Lizzie,' the woman said, her voice shaky. 'She cried out; then she started to cough, said she couldn't breathe and she felt dizzy and sick.'

'Looks like an allergic reaction to me. Is she allergic to anything?'

'Not as far as I know.'

'But she cried out. Maybe she was stung,' Tom suggested. He pointed out a red patch on Lizzie's arm. 'That looks like a wasp sting.'

'Has Lizzie ever been stung before?' Amy asked the child's mother.

'Yes, but she didn't react like this.'

'You don't, the first time,' Amy said, rummaging in her handbag for her mobile phone. 'Is anyone in the family allergic to wasp stings?'

'No.'

'Are there any other medical conditions we need to know about—asthma or anything?' Tom asked.

'No, she's always been really healthy.'

Amy gave her mobile phone to Perdy. 'Perdy, call the ambulance and tell them where we are and that we have a little girl with an anaphylactic reaction to a sting.' She turned to Tom, about to ask him to check Lizzie's airway and pulse, to discover that he was already doing it.

'I'm going to give her some adrenalin,' Amy told Lizzie's mother, 'because that's going to help stop the swelling and make it easier for her to breathe. What happens with allergic reactions is your body produces lots of histamine. The histamine makes all your blood vessels go wider and leaky, so that makes all the tissues around them swell—that's what's happening to Lizzie right now. The adrenalin stops her body making more histamine, which will help open her airways; the adrenalin will make her blood vessels go narrower again so the swelling goes down.'

'Airway clear,' Tom said, 'but her pulse is a bit low. Let's help you sit up, sweetheart, so you can breathe more easily. Big breath in for me, that's right, and then slowly let it out. One, two, three—that's brilliant. Keep doing that for me.' He turned to Amy. 'Did you say you have adrenalin on you?'

'I'm allergic to wasp stings myself so, yes, I have a pen and I carry it everywhere.' She took the adrenalin pen from her bag and removed the cap; then she pressed the tip into the child's thigh muscle until it popped and held it there for a ten seconds, counting under her breath. Then she removed the pen and massaged the area for another few seconds; all the time, Tom was talking to the child and her mother and soothing them. Finally, Amy put the cap back on the pen and shoved it back in her bag.

'The ambulance is on its way,' Perdy reported, handing the phone back to Amy. 'I told them where we were and that I'd be waving a pink towel over my head as soon as I see them—I'll go and get my towel.'

'Thanks, Perdy, you're a star.' Amy hugged her. 'That's a brilliant idea.'

'Is she going to be all right?' Lizzie's mother asked.

'Lots of people have severe allergic reactions to wasps,' Amy reassured her. 'Give the adrenalin a few minutes and she'll start to brighten up a bit—but she's going to need to carry a pen like this with her in future, and make sure she has the instructions with her as well. Some people like to wear a bracelet to warn people they have a medical condition.'

'And then it's a matter of trying to avoid wasps,' Tom said. 'Make sure she doesn't go near bins in summer, and don't let her have sugary drinks outdoors—especially cans, because wasps have a habit of crawling into drink cans.'

'Also make sure she doesn't walk barefoot on grass, and avoid really bright clothes because they attract wasps,' Amy added. 'And always, always have the adrenalin pen with you.'

'Is she always going to be allergic to wasps?' the little girl's mother asked.

'Sometimes children grow out of it, and she can have desensitisation injections,' Tom said.

'Though it's a long course, takes five years, and has to be done in a specialist centre in case of a severe reaction,' Amy explained. 'For now, they'll check her over in hospital and finish the treatment there. Is there anyone we can call for you?'

'My husband's at work.' She sighed. 'We thought we'd just have a nice day on the beach, a picnic and what have you.'

'You weren't to know that Lizzie's allergic to wasp stings,' Amy said gently.

By the time the woman had called her husband, Perdy was waving the pink towel over her head. Tom briefed the paramedics on what they'd done; they listened to Lizzie's chest and checked her blood pressure, then put her on an oxygen mask and swiftly inserted an IV line.

'The mask's to help her breathe more easily,' Tom explained as Lizzie's mother blanched.

'And the line in her hand means that if they need to give her some medication, they can do it quickly,' Amy added.

'Thank you so much for helping. If it hadn't been for you...' She choked back a sob.

Amy patted her shoulder. 'We were here, so don't torment yourself with the might-have-beens.'

'Is that little girl going to be all right?' Perdy asked as the ambulance drove away.

'She'll be fine,' Tom reassured her.

'If she has a second reaction, they'll have all the drugs they need to give her,' Amy added. 'And I need to remember to get another pen to replace this one.'

'I can sort that out for you at the surgery,' Tom said. 'Was that your only one?'

'No, I always carry two, just in case.'

'You two were brilliant—Dad sorting the breathing and you doing the questions between you—like a real team,' Perdy said.

Tom and Amy exchanged loaded glances.

Could they be a team? Amy wondered.

'You could be the same sort of doctor as Dad, Amy,' Perdy said, 'if you didn't want to go back to the hospital.'

Amy smiled. 'Maybe. Though it's not quite that simple; I'd have to retrain. It'd be quite a big step, if I decided to take it.'

'Was Joseph your sort of doctor?' Perdy asked curiously.

'They didn't really know much about nerves back in those days,' Amy said, 'and they definitely didn't do the kind of operations that I do. They didn't have X-rays and they weren't even sure about the structures of the body. But I guess Joseph was at the cutting edge of medicine back then—I know he was definitely there at the first operation involving anaesthetic.'

'So he was like you, then.'

'Except he was married, with six children.'

'Do you want to get married and have children?' Perdy asked.

For once, Tom didn't step in and distract her. Amy had no idea what Tom had said to Perdy—had he broached the subject over the weekend, asked Perdy how she would feel if he started dating someone? 'I don't know,' she said. 'Maybe. Now, about this moat...'

'You're quiet,' Amy said later that evening, when Perdy was asleep and she was curled up on the sofa in the conservatory with Tom.

'Thinking,' he said. 'About today. You were spot on when you treated that little girl.'

'Because I know the drill.'

'The point is,' Tom said softly, 'you went straight in there and you made all the right decisions. No hesitation, no worrying about things—you acted on instinct.'

She wriggled out of his arms and sat up, crossing her legs. 'And your point is?'

'Maybe it's time you cut yourself a bit of slack,' he said, 'and started trusting yourself again. I know you said you weren't sure if you wanted to go back to neurology, but from what I've seen of your work you're an excellent doctor. You're good with patients, you're good with relatives, and it'd be a real waste if you gave it all up.'

'Maybe.' Amy shrugged.

'Definitely,' he corrected gently. 'Trust your instincts, Amy. They won't lead you wrong.'

Wouldn't they?

'I know it's none of my business, but I—' He stopped abruptly. 'We're friends,' he said.

'Yes,' Amy said, wondering what he'd been going to say at first. That he cared about her, maybe?

'And friends look out for each other. Give advice.'

'Uh-huh.' Just where was he going with this?

'I think you should take Marty up on the pain clinic. It'll help our patients—and it'll help you, too.'

'Maybe,' Amy said again.

He shifted so his arms were round her again. 'I'm sorry if I've overstepped the boundaries. Yet again.' He kissed her gently. 'I just want you to believe in yourself again. Because I believe in you, Amy.'

And Amy had to bite back the tears. He believed in her. So why couldn't she believe in herself, too?

CHAPTER ELEVEN

ON Monday morning, Amy dropped by the surgery to see Marty.

'My dear girl, it's lovely to see you.' He greeted her with a hug. 'What can I do for you?'

'It's more what I can do for you. If you still want me to do that pain clinic, I will.'

'We'd all be delighted to have you on board,' he said warmly. 'When's a good time for you?'

She smiled. 'Whenever. My time's my own at the moment.'

He flicked into a screen on his computer. 'How about Wednesday morning? Say, ten until one?'

'Fine. I take it you have patients in mind?'

'There won't be any problems filling the slots,' Marty said.

'And I can prescribe from here, or book sessions with a physio, or refer patients to a surgical team?' Amy asked.

Marty smiled. 'Of course. And I'll make sure all the admin side of things is sorted before you start.'

'Thank you.' She paused. 'Um, Marty, I'll only be here for a month. I could do a training session for the GPs, if you like, about triaging back pain. I mean, I know you all know the red flags and what to look out for, but if a re-fresher would be helpful and I wouldn't be treading on anyone's toes…'

'That'd be very helpful,' Marty said. 'And if you can include the gamma knife stuff, that'll help us all to keep up to date. I'll find out when everyone's free, shall I, and let you know?'

'Great. And if you can get me a connection for my laptop to a large TV screen, I can do you a proper presen-tation with diagrams.'

'Better than that,' Marty said. 'June's the head of the primary school now. There's a big government thing at the moment about how schools have to be "extended" and offer services to the community, so we can borrow a classroom with an interactive whiteboard—and if you put your pre-sentation on a memory stick, June can load it up for you.'

'Marty, I never knew you were such a wheeler-dealer.'

'It helps us,' Marty said, 'and it helps June—it's evidence for her report that she's offering things to the community. Plus, of course, it helps school funds. But don't get her started on that.'

On Wednesday morning, just before her first clinic, Amy felt even more nervous than she had when she'd first started as a neurologist; but when her first patient walked in, clearly in pain, her training kicked in and everything seemed to flow.

In the fifteen-minute break scheduled between the two batches of patients, Tom brought her a coffee. 'How's it going?' he asked.

She took a risk and kissed him; the surprise and pleasure in his eyes sent a warm glow through her. 'It's great. You were right—this is something I needed to do.' And the fact that he'd believed in her, even when she hadn't been able to believe in herself, really helped.

'Good. While you're in grateful mode, there's something I want to ask you.'

'What?'

'I have a patient with lumbar canal stenosis. He's going to have an op, and he's coming in tomorrow to chat to me about it.'

'And you want me to talk him through it?' she guessed.

He spread his hands. 'You were brilliant with Mrs Cooper.'

'All right. Joe still has his skeleton,' she said thoughtfully, 'but I might need you as a model. You might have to strip.'

His eyes glittered. 'Oh, yes?'

'Just to the waist. So I can point out bits on your back.'

His smile broadened. 'Sure. And if you want me to strip for you later—the full monty—it'll be my pleasure. Or, even better...' he nuzzled the sensitive spot just behind her ear '...you can take my clothes off for me.'

She felt herself flush. 'Tom Ashby, you can't proposition me like that at work!' But she was laughing as he stole another kiss and left her consulting room.

The clinic had made her realise how much she'd missed medicine, being part of a team and helping people. And maybe Tom was right; maybe she really did have a future in medicine.

On Thursday morning, Amy joined Tom in his consulting room to see Mr Garson, his patient with lumbar canal stenosis.

With Eloise being an emergency specialist, Tom had never worked with her as a team; but Amy's specialty was different, and Tom loved the idea of working with her to help a patient.

Tom introduced her to Mr Garson, then sat back to let

Amy do the talking, prepared to step in with additional information where she needed it.

Amy had her laptop screen slanted so that Mr Garson could see it. 'This is a picture of the lower part of your spinal canal. As you get older, the space narrows—as does the space between the discs in your spine—so when you move the bones pinch the nerves in your spine, and that's what's causing the pain.'

'Some days are better than others,' Mr Garson said, 'but I can't walk as well as I could. My legs hurt and go weak.' He grimaced. 'And whoever said Norfolk's flat hasn't walked down the cliff road.'

'Do you find it's easier to walk uphill than downhill?' Amy asked.

'Yes.'

'And it's better when you sit down, lean forward or put your foot up on a stool?'

He nodded. 'I can't lie down to play trains with my grandson, though. Hurts like mad if I lie on my tummy.'

'And the treatment so far hasn't worked?'

'Painkillers, physio, and then a combination of bed rest to reduce the inflammation followed by light activity,' Tom confirmed. 'No, they haven't.'

'May I look at your X-rays?' Amy asked.

Mr Garson gave his consent, and Tom brought up the images on his computer.

'Can you see these lumps here?' Amy pointed them out. 'These are called osteophytes—they're bony spurs that your body can develop with age. They definitely need to be removed. So you're booked in for a laminectomy?'

'And I have to admit I'm not looking forward to it,' Mr Garson said.

'Lots of patients say the same—until they come round

and discover that the pain's gone,' Amy said reassuringly. She brought another diagram up onto the screen. 'If you see these bones here—your surgeon will trim the bony arch, and that takes the pressure off the nerves, so the pain will go.'

'But if you're taking the bone away, won't it mean that the bones are weaker?' Mr Garson asked.

'No. I suppose it's a bit like if you have a door that sticks, you plane the edge off so it stops sticking against the frame,' Amy said.

Tom loved the way she explained things—just as she'd used the example of the tripod on a camera to describe the head frame for gamma knife surgery, this made it so much easier for the patient to relate to and took a lot of the fear away. Amy was brilliant with patients, and he could see exactly why she'd become a consultant relatively quickly.

At this point he was half expecting her to ask him to take his shirt off to act as a model, but clearly she'd been teasing him because instead she explained about the MRI scan to Mr Garson.

'It's a very common operation,' she reassured him, 'and your surgeon will have done quite a few of them, so try not to worry.'

'But my back won't crumble?'

'It won't crumble,' Amy reassured him. 'And you'll be out of bed the day after surgery with the help of physiotherapists. We like to get you moving as soon as possible because it will help you recover more quickly.'

'Will it hurt?' he asked.

'Yes, at first, but you'll have painkillers to get you started and it will get easier every day. And the really good news is that the pain in your leg will be either a lot better or completely gone, straight away.'

'And how long do I have to stay in hospital?'

'Usually it's a few days,' Amy said. 'When you go home, it's a good idea to make sure it's in a car with a reclining seat so you can lie back. I use dissolvable stitches, but if your surgeon doesn't, you'll go back to have the stitches out in ten days.'

'It'll take you about six weeks to recover and you absolutely mustn't lift anything,' Tom added.

'But keep as mobile as possible to help yourself heal,' Amy said. 'I'd recommend taking showers rather than a bath for the first couple of weeks. You'll also have some further physiotherapy, which is likely to start about three weeks after the op, and you'll be back to see your surgeon in Outpatients about six weeks later.'

'How long will I be off work?' Mr Garson asked.

'What do you do?'

'I'm a postman.'

'So that's a lot of walking and lifting.' Amy grimaced. 'Not for at least three months, possibly four. Do you play any sport?'

'Rugby.'

'Absolutely not, for six months after the op—it puts too much strain on your spine,' Amy explained.

'And, um…me and the wife?' Colour stained his cheeks.

Tom came to his rescue. 'About three weeks, but you need a position that won't put pressure on your back.'

'And don't arch your spine,' Amy added. 'Is there anything else that you've been worrying about? Even if you think it's something little or silly, please ask, because I'd much rather have a patient who isn't worried, and I know my colleagues all feel the same.'

'I think that's it,' Mr Garson said. 'You've made it all so clear. I can tell the wife and she won't be worrying quite so much.'

When he'd closed the consulting-room door behind him, Tom said softly, 'Thank you. You were brilliant.'

She shrugged off the compliment. 'It's one of the most common ops.'

'Even so. He was worried sick, and you've taken a huge weight off him.'

'Good. Well, I'll see you later. Are you in surgery this afternoon?'

'No. So if you're free for lunch...may I have the pleasure of your company?'

She nodded. 'I'd like that.'

'Good. And, Amy?'

'Yes?'

He kissed her lightly. 'That's on account.'

She grinned. 'I'll hold you to that, Dr Ashby.'

Tom concentrated on his patients for the rest of the morning, but all the way home he thought of Amy. He loved the quickness of her mind, her gentleness, her sudden grin and the unexpected flare of mischief in her eyes. And he couldn't wait to see her again, listen to her telling him about her day and then telling her about his.

Then it hit him.

He'd broken all the rules.

He'd fallen in love with Amy.

Part of him felt guilty about it. He shouldn't be feeling this way so soon after Eloise; it had only been a year. And yet Amy, with her huge heart and her innate kindness, had brought so much light, so much joy into his life. Perdy's, too. He wanted it to stay that way.

She'd admitted that she'd missed him when he'd gone away. And she'd trusted him enough to tell him about her past. But, given her experiences with Colin, would she be able to trust him that bit further, in time, and become a family with him and Perdy?

Amy was working on the casebooks when he returned, and he made them both a sandwich while she finished the section she'd just started.

'Thanks,' she said, kissing him as she joined him at the table.

'How's it going?' he asked.

'I'm enjoying it. And I think Joseph was having a good time because his writing's relaxed instead of cramped with worry.'

'So how much of your sabbatical do you have left—six weeks?'

'Something like that,' she said.

'And then you're going back to London?'

She toyed with her sandwich. 'I don't know. Though I am starting to miss work. You're right, Tom: a doctor is who I am and what I want to be. It's just a matter of whether I can trust myself again.'

He reached over to squeeze her hand. 'From what I've seen of you, you're a good doctor. Follow your instincts: they won't let you down, and you're not going to let yourself down. But...'

'But?'

'Maybe,' he said, 'it might be worth trying working in a different hospital, one where you don't have memories to haunt you and bring back all the doubts.'

'That's a very good point,' she said, squeezing his hand back. 'Thanks, Tom. You've really helped.'

Was that more he could see in her eyes, or was he just wishing it was there?

But now wasn't the right time to push. The last thing he wanted was to make her back away. He needed the right place and the right time to ask her if she'd consider staying near him. Of course Perdy had to come first—there was no question about that. But he was pretty sure that Perdy liked Amy enough to want her to stay in their lives.

Sure, it was greedy of him to want everything, but with Amy in his life there was a good chance he could have everything he'd always wanted: an equal partner who'd put their family first, just as he did. Someone who loved him as much as he loved her.

He couldn't tell her in words.

But he could tell her another way.

And when they'd finished lunch, he drew her hand up to his mouth, keeping his gaze fixed on hers, and kissed each knuckle in turn. Her eyes widened as he pressed his tongue against the pulse beating madly in her wrist; and that crazy tattoo told him she wanted this as much as he did. He continued kissing his way up her arm to the sensitive spot in the crook of her elbow, then pulled her onto his lap so she was sitting astride him.

The next thing he knew, her hands were tangled in his hair and she was kissing him with the same hunger that seared deep inside him. He untucked her shirt from her jeans and flattened his palms against her midriff; she shifted so that her sex was pressed against his. The soft denim was way too much of a barrier for his liking—and so was the fragile lace of her bra. He slid one hand up her back, smoothing his palm against her spine, then unsnapped her bra and pushed the material out of the way so he could cup her breasts.

I love you, he said silently, willing her to realise it.

Right at that moment, he really needed to feel her body wrapped round his. Impatience made his fingers clumsy and he couldn't undo one of the buttons of her shirt; he tugged, and it pinged off. The sound brought him back to his senses. 'Amy, I'm so sorry,' he began. 'I shouldn't have—'

'If you hadn't done it, I would've done,' she told him, her voice low and husky, 'because I'm going crazy here, Tom. I need to feel you against me.'

Desire spun through him again. His fingers tangled with hers as together they removed her shirt; he heard her sharp intake of breath as the pad of his thumb brushed against her nipples, and he felt her nipples hardening under his touch, telling him that she wanted this as much as he did.

He drew a line of kisses along her shoulder; he loved the taste of her skin, the warmth and softness beneath his mouth. She clearly liked it, too, as she tipped her head to one side, offering him more, and wriggled closer.

'Tom, please.'

There was the same neediness in her voice that was dragging through him. He kissed the curve of her neck, lingered in the hollows of her collarbones, and felt her shiver as finally he took one nipple into his mouth and sucked.

'Oh, oh, *yes*, Tom.' She slid her fingers into his hair and drew him closer.

He teased her with his lips and his tongue until he could feel her breathing becoming more uneven.

She tugged his shirt out of his jeans. 'I need to touch you,' she whispered as he lifted his head.

'Do it,' he said softly.

She fumbled with the buttons of his shirt and pushed the garment off his shoulders before splaying her hands across his pectorals. 'You're so beautiful, Tom.'

'So are you.' He stole a kiss, all the while thinking, And I love you. This was more than just sating a sexual urge.

'I need you,' she said, and slid off his lap. 'Right now.'

She took his hand and he let her lead him up to her

bedroom. He closed the door behind them and pulled her back into his arms, kissing her deeply; she shivered.

He dragged his mouth from hers. 'Are you OK?'

'More than OK. I love the feel of your skin against mine.'

'That makes two of us.'

He slowly unpeeled the rest of her clothes from her body, stroking every millimetre of skin as he uncovered it. Over the last few weeks he'd grown to know where she liked being touched and how. He knew her body as intimately as he knew his own—and he knew he wanted to be with her always. He just had to find the right way of asking her without scaring her away.

It took him a matter of seconds to strip off his own clothes; then he lifted her up and laid her on the bed. He kissed his way down her body, exploring her with his mouth as he had with his hands, enjoying the way she made tiny little noises of pleasure and wriggled against him.

'Tom, now,' she whispered. 'I'm going crazy here. I need you inside me.'

And he needed to be there too.

He grabbed a condom from his wallet, dealt with it swiftly, and then at last he was right where he wanted to be—losing himself in her. With Amy, he felt complete, more than he ever had with Eloise. Guilt flooded through him at the thought, but it was washed away by desire when she kissed him fiercely.

This felt so right.

I love you, he said inside his head as he eased into her.

I love you, he said silently again as he felt her body began to ripple round his, the little involuntary tightenings as she reached her own climax and tipped him over the edge to his.

I love you.

CHAPTER TWELVE

OVER the next week, Amy did two further clinics at the surgery. The more time she spent with patients, the more she realised that she was ready to go back. Tom had been right to push her into doing the pain clinic; it had given her confidence the final boost it needed.

She also thought that Tom was right about something else—that she needed to work somewhere without any memories.

Not only that: going back to her old job in London would mean leaving Tom and Perdy, something she really didn't want to do. She'd learned over the last few weeks that she needed more than just a job: she wanted love and a family in her life, too. And that meant Tom and Perdy. She knew she'd fallen in love with them; and she thought—hoped—that they felt the same way. Tom hadn't said anything, but when they made love she was sure that she saw something in his eyes.

Unless maybe she was hoping so hard that she was seeing what she wanted to see rather than what was actually there.

Then again, he'd told her something she'd never heard from anyone else. *I believe in you.*

From Tom—a man who'd loved his late wife but had

never felt he was enough for her—that was tantamount to a declaration.

Trust your instincts. They won't lead you wrong.

And her instincts were telling her to stay here. To take that risk. To be a family with Tom and Perdy.

She logged onto the internet and checked the 'situations vacant' pages on the local hospital trust websites; she was surprised and delighted to discover that there were opportunities in her specialty. Maybe only as a locum at first, but there were possibilities.

Which meant that now was the time to take the next step.

She glanced at the clock. With luck, she'd be able to catch her boss just before he headed to a lecture. Swiftly, she dialled his number and Della put her through.

'Amy! How are you doing?' he asked.

'Fine, thanks. And you?'

'Fine. So what can I do for you?'

'I just wanted you to know that I've finally got my head together now,' she said.

'You certainly sound brighter,' he said, sounding approving.

'And I want to carry on as a neurologist.'

'Are you sure you're ready to come back?' he asked.

'That's the thing, Fergus.' She bit her lip. 'I feel horrible asking this, especially as you've been so good to me, but I think I want to stay right here. Would you consider giving me a reference if I applied for a job locally?'

'I don't particularly want to lose one of my brightest stars,' Fergus said, 'but if it's what you really want, then of course I'll give you a reference. But make sure it's really what you want. Don't rush into anything, OK?'

'I promise. I'm not rushing—I'm really ready to go back to work.'

'I'd much rather have you back in my department,' Fergus said, 'because you're not going to be easy to replace. But if you really want to move hospitals, and it'll make you happy, you have my blessing.'

'Thank you, Fergus,' she said. 'I owe you so much.'

'Not at all. You've been wonderful to work with. But don't you dare go poaching any of my staff when you become senior consultant. Especially young Danny. I want him here for at least the next five years, OK?'

She laughed. 'OK.'

When she'd ended the call, she rang up about the three nearest jobs then emailed her CV and Fergus's contact details as a reference. It might come to nothing, she just had to hope she'd be lucky.

And once she had something firmer to consider, she could sit down with Tom. Talk it over with him. And see where the future lay.

The following Thursday, Amy was just about to take a break for lunch when her mobile phone started ringing. She frowned. She wasn't expecting a call; it would be early in the morning where her parents were and very late at night for Joe and Cassie. Her heart missed a beat: please, don't say there was something wrong with Beth or the baby? She glanced at the screen, and was truly shocked to see the name and photograph on display.

Not her parents; not Joe and Cassie. Not Tom, calling between patients to see if she would be free for lunch.

Laura.

Her heart began to thud and for a moment Amy didn't dare to answer it. But then she took a deep breath, pressed the button and whispered, 'Hello?'

'Amy? It's Laura.'

Laura sounded just as nervous and unsure as Amy herself felt. 'Yes.' She willed herself to stay calm. 'How are you?' Then she sighed. 'Sorry, that was a stupid question. Laura, I'm so sorry about what happened.'

'So am I. And I'm so sorry that I've taken everything out on you.'

Amy couldn't quite believe what she was hearing. 'What?'

'Where are you, Amy? I couldn't get an answer from your landline, so I rang you at the hospital and they said you were taking a sabbatical.'

Of sorts. And Amy knew that Laura was the last person to whom she could explain the reason why she was taking a break from her job. 'I'm at Joe and Cassie's.'

'How are they?'

'Fine. They're over in Australia.'

'Seeing Beth?'

'And the new baby—their first grandchild.'

'Beth's had a baby?' Laura sounded shocked.

Well, they hadn't been speaking since October. Of course Laura wouldn't know anything about the baby. 'Nearly a month ago—a little boy, Samuel Joseph, nearly four kilos. He's seriously cute: Cassie's emailed me some pictures, and so has Beth. Mum and baby are both doing well, and Joe and Cassie are just thrilled.'

'So you're house-sitting for them?'

'Yes.' Amy's chest felt tight and she knew that asking the question burning inside her could mean the end of the phone call, but how could she not ask? 'How's Ben?'

'That's why I'm calling.'

Amy's knees suddenly felt as if they'd dissolved and the back of her neck felt hot. Oh, God. Please don't say Ben was worse. Or—she could hardly bear to think the word—dead.

'Amy? Are you still there?'

'Yes,' she whispered.

'He's—he's…'

Amy could tell that her best friend was crying; it must be bad news. Tears were pricking her own eyes—and she felt so helpless, so useless. She should be there in London, holding Laura and telling her she'd get through this and supporting her every step of the way. 'I'm so, so sorry,' she said. 'I know why you haven't wanted to see me and I completely understand, but if I can help you through this now, all you have to do is say and I'll get in the car right now and drive straight to you.'

'No.'

A flat rejection. She swallowed hard. Well, what had she had expected?

'I mean not now, you don't have to rush back.' Laura's breath hitched. 'Amy, Ben can move his hands fully again.'

Amy sat down heavily. 'He can move his hands? When did this happen?'

'A month ago. He woke me up in the middle of the night to show me. I was so scared… Amy, if it had been temporary, he would've been destroyed. But he can really move his hands again. And day by day he's been able to move his arms and shoulders a little bit more.' She gulped. 'He's able to do some things for himself again, he won't have to keep relying on me or a carer. I know he's never going to be able to walk again, and he's never going to be able to ride again, but he can write, use a computer, call people on the phone. He's getting some of his life back. He can still be part of the stables.'

'That's fantastic news. Oh, Laura, I'm so glad.' Though there was something else she needed to know. 'How's the pain?'

'It's always going to be there, but he's managing better

now. And so am I.' She paused. 'Amy, Ben and I…we were so unfair to you, blaming you for everything. We were wrong, and I'm sorry.'

'I don't blame you for acting the way you did. I was the one who screwed up.'

'You didn't screw up, Amy. The doctors we've seen since—they explained the way the spine and the nerves work. I mean, I know you explained it to us at the time, but we were both so shocked we didn't take it in properly—and then we were so overwhelmed with misery, at the way everything had gone down the tubes and things looked so impossible for us… We took it out on you, and we shouldn't have done.'

'But I couldn't fix the damage,' Amy said. 'I failed you both.'

'You did everything you could—more than a lot of surgeons could've done. If it hadn't been for you, Ben wouldn't have been able to move even his fingers.'

'He couldn't move his fingers when—' When Laura had said she never, ever wanted to see her again. The words stuck in Amy's throat.

'The doctors say it's like that sometimes—it just needed time for things to settle down again and heal enough for us to see the full extent of the damage.'

Exactly what Amy had tried to tell Laura and Ben herself, but they'd refused to listen. And the longer Laura had stayed out of touch, the more certain Amy had been that the nerves hadn't settled down and Ben hadn't recovered any more movement. That she'd ruined their lives.

After Ben had been discharged from the London Victoria, his treatment had been done at a hospital much nearer to where he and Laura lived, so Amy hadn't even been able to find out how he was through the grapevine at work. Not that her colleagues would have breached any confidential medical detail, but if he'd stayed at the London Victoria she would at least have been able to get a rough idea of how Ben and Laura were.

'So they're saying it's a T1 injury, not a C8?'

'Yes. And it's because of you that it's a T1. We both owe you so much. With Ben getting some mobility back, it's taken so much pressure off us. Both of us can see things more clearly now. And we might even be able to have...' Her voice tailed off. 'Well, it's early days,' she said briskly.

But Amy knew exactly what Laura was talking about. A baby. Laura's biological clock had started ticking loudly in the months before Ben's accident. It was one of the reasons why his spinal injury had been such a blow: Ben had lost his career, his mobility, and maybe the chance of ever being a father. Now, it seemed, there was hope. They'd need help, but perhaps it was no longer completely out of the question.

It would have been seriously tough for Laura to cope with a tetraplegic husband and a newborn. But if Ben regained the full use of his arms, hands and upper body, he'd be able to help her with the baby.

'Amy...I've missed you so much,' Laura said.

Exactly how Amy herself had felt, at losing her best friend—practically her sister. And to hear the words she never, ever thought she'd hear... It broke her. She choked back a sob.

'Amy?'

'I've missed you, too—and I've hated myself for not supporting you, the way you supported me when my world collapsed after Colin.' She swallowed hard. 'I should've been there for you.'

'How could you, when I pushed you away and told you never to darken my doorstep again?'

'As your best friend, I could've ignored that. But how could I comfort you, when I was the one who'd wrecked your life, when everything was a mess and it was all my fault?'

'I was wrong about that. And it wasn't your fault.' Laura was crying openly now. 'I miss you, Amy. And I want to see you. When are you coming back to London?'

'I don't know. A month, maybe.' And even then maybe not for long.

'A month? So what exactly are you doing on this sabbatical?'

'Joseph's casebooks.'

'Amy, your family's been talking about doing something with them for years. Why now?'

'It seemed like a good idea.' How could she tell Laura how bad things had been? She knew that Laura had had it much, much harder. Laura was the one who had to live with the consequences of Ben's accident.

'There's something you're not telling me,' Laura said, perceptive as always.

'I'm fine,' Amy lied.

'Amy, you're bawling your eyes out.'

'So are you.' She dragged in a breath. 'I've missed you so much, Laura. You and Ben.'

'I'm so, so sorry I hurt you.'

'You were hurting, too,' Amy pointed out. 'And you had it worse than I did.'

'I was so angry. And I was wrong. How am I ever going to make it up to you?'

'You don't need to,' Amy said. 'You're my best friend. The fact you're actually talking to me... I'm just so glad to hear your voice. And to hear that Ben's getting better.'

'He's never going to walk again,' Laura said. 'I know that.' And there were other complications that could set in,

Amy knew. Not that this was the right time to talk about it. There would be time to talk about it later. Face to face.

'But I can deal with it now. It's like having my future back.'

'I'm so happy for you, Laura. And you know I'll help in any way I can.'

'I know. Right now, just talking to you is enough.'

This was the call Amy had dreamed about but had thought would never, ever happen. And when she finally put the phone down again, she curled up in the chair and cried her eyes out—all the pain and misery, just letting it go.

Buster put his paws on her knees and nosed her anxiously; she wrapped her arms round him and sobbed until all the heartbreak was out.

At last the tears stopped, and she made a fuss of the dog. 'Sorry, boy. I didn't mean to bawl all over you.' She headed for her bathroom, washed her face and bathed her swollen eyes. It felt as if the last part of the burden had been lifted off her shoulders; all these months of misery, when she'd doubted every bit of her own ability, had simply melted away—thanks to Tom's belief in her, and now having Laura and Ben's forgiveness.

And now she was really ready to move on. To face the future…with a smile.

CHAPTER THIRTEEN

LATER that evening, after Perdy had gone to bed, Tom was sitting in the garden with Amy. There was definitely something different about her, but he couldn't put his finger on it. Her hair was the same colour, she wasn't wearing anything different—but that haunted look in her eyes had vanished, and she was smiling more than usual.

She sparkled.

'You look happy,' he said. 'Good day?'

She nodded. 'I've had some great news. Laura rang me today.'

Given that Amy was smiling, that had to be a good thing. The beginning of mending the rift between them. 'So it all went OK?'

'Yes.' Her smile broadened. 'Ben's finally healing, and he's got some movement back in his hands. He's still never going to walk again, but he's going to be more independent. With a bit of help from physio…well, they're going to get more of their lives back.'

'That's fantastic.' For her. Of course it was. And he was genuinely pleased for her; but at the same time he suddenly felt hollow. What did this mean for their relationship—their future? 'I'm really pleased,' he made himself say. 'So that proves you did do the right thing in that op.'

'Mmm.' She looked rueful. 'I've learned my lesson, though. In future, I won't get emotionally involved.'

The hollow feeling grew stronger. She didn't just mean in her career, did she? he thought. She meant in her life, too. And now she'd go back to her career in London. She'd choose her job over him and Perdy, just as Eloise had. He'd been stupid to hope that their relationship had started to mean as much to her as it did to him. Stupid to hope that maybe she might be able to love him back in the way that he loved her. The doubts all came crowding back in. He and Perdy hadn't been enough for Eloise; why would they be enough for Amy?

'Uh-huh,' he said.

She frowned. 'Tom? What's up?'

'Nothing.' He paused. 'So when are you going back to London?'

'I'm not sure if I am.'

He blinked. 'Why not? You're a neurosurgeon. A consultant. High-powered. And now you've got your confidence back, why wouldn't you go back to London—back to the job you spent years training to do?'

'Because I've had a lot of time to think about what I really want. Yes, I love my job, just as you love yours. But it isn't the whole of who I am. And I don't want to come home to my empty flat every night any more.' She took a deep breath. 'I haven't been in denial about it, exactly, but I know now that I've been suppressing what I really want and telling myself that my job's enough to fill my life. It isn't.'

Hope flared inside him. 'So what do you want, Amy?'

'I want a family,' she said. 'And I don't mean as a substitute for Colin and Millie. I want a family of my own.'

The flame went out again. A family of her own. 'Someone without any complications,' he said.

She shook her head. 'Families aren't simple. And for someone so bright, you can be incredibly dense, Dr Ashby. Unless...' She bit her lip. 'Unless I've got it all completely wrong and I've been deluding myself again, the same way I did about Colin.'

He couldn't quite take in what she was saying. Did she mean that she wanted him and Perdy? 'Deluding yourself about what?'

'You, me and Perdy,' she said. 'Tom, I know you're still mourning Eloise and your feelings about her are complicated. I know these things take time. I know we said we'd help each other out of a bad place and we weren't going to get involved. And I don't want to rush you into something you're not ready for. But I was hoping that maybe...' She raked a hand through her hair. 'Oh, God, why are these things so hard to say?'

'Hoping that maybe...?' he prompted.

'That maybe things have changed for you these last few weeks, the way they have for me. That you'd be prepared to take a chance on me. That I could share your life and be a family with you and Perdy.'

Yes. That was everything he wanted, too. And yet... 'What about your job? I can't see how you'd want to give up working in a London hospital, at the cutting edge of your specialty. And Perdy's settled here. I don't want to uproot her yet again and drag her back to London.' He blew out a breath. 'The obvious compromise is that you work in London and we come and stay at weekends, but that...' He grimaced.

'That isn't being a family,' Amy agreed. 'And you don't have to uproot Perdy, because I can still do the same job outside London. I, um, took the liberty of talking to my boss last week. He'll give me a reference. And I've checked out the local opportunities.'

'Local?' Tom blinked.

She nodded. 'I knew I wanted to go back to work—but I also knew I didn't want to leave you and Perdy. So I thought I'd find out what my options were.' She looked slightly shy. 'I was planning to talk it over with you when I heard back—see what you thought. It looks as if there's a fair chance I could get a locum job, and maybe it'll lead to something permanent.'

'And that would really be enough for you?'

'Having everything, you mean?' She gave him a quirky smile. 'Yeah, I reckon.'

Tom swallowed hard. 'Amy. There's a bit of me that wants to pick you up and twirl you round and yell to the skies how much I love you.'

'And what about the other bit of you?'

The bit that was panicking. How could he tell her that without sounding insulting? 'Full of questions.' He owed it to her to be honest. He took her hand. 'And full of doubts.'

'You think Perdy won't be happy about it?'

'Far from it. I'm pretty sure she'd be delighted,' Tom said. 'She likes you—really likes you. When she's with me and you're not around, she never stops talking about you.' And he'd already fallen hard for Amy. He just about managed to stop himself yanking her into his arms and kissing her senseless. 'Amy, I want to be with you, too. I fell for you a long time ago. Not when I first met you, though I found you attractive—it was when you let your barriers down and I started getting to know you. You're everything I want in a life partner. I can talk to you about anything, I like being with you, and you're the sexiest woman I've ever met.'

'But?'

She'd picked up on it without him having to say the words—she was that much in tune with him. So he really hoped she'd understand what he was trying to say now. 'But I've been here before and it was a disaster,' he said softly. 'I was married to a high-powered doctor, and Perdy and I turned out not to be enough for her. And even though I know you're not Eloise and I love you, there's still a bit of me that's terrified in case we're not enough for you either. What happens six months, a year down the line? What happens if you get bored and discover you need more, the way Eloise did?'

Amy looked steadily at him. 'I made a family with someone who changed his mind. Bits of me are scared too that the same thing's going to happen again—I mean, I know it's not physically possible for you to go back to Eloise, but what's to stop you having second thoughts and realising that I'm not good enough to be her substitute?'

'You're not her substitute,' Tom said. 'And it's not a question of not being good enough. You and Eloise are different people. You see things in different ways. And,' he pointed out, 'I'm not Colin.'

'I know that. And you know I'm not Eloise.' Amy's eyes were very clear. 'My background's similar to hers, but I do know the difference between trying to please someone who can't be pleased and reaching out for what I really want. And I don't want the same things Eloise wanted. I want so very much more: I want you and Perdy.'

The lump in Tom's throat was too huge for him to speak.

'You've helped me see that I'm a neurosurgeon and I wouldn't be happy doing anything else,' Amy continued, 'but at the end of the day it's my job and it's only part of who I am. I need more than that to make me whole. I want a home, Tom. A home with a proper family, a solid base where there's a slot especially shaped for me to fit into. I want a little girl who gives me a hug when she gets home from school and tells me about her day. I want a husband who shares his life with me—his hopes, his dreams, his fears. I want to be part of a team, a proper family.' Her eyes glittered. 'I want all that, Tom. And I want it with you and Perdy.'

He still couldn't speak. So he wrapped his arms round her and kissed her, pouring his soul into the kiss. And when he finally broke it and looked into her eyes, he knew she understood.

'I love you, Amy,' he said softly.

'I love you, too. And I know you're going to have doubts about this—just as I will—but we'll talk about them. Deal with them together and not let them get in the way.'

'Agreed.' He paused. 'So, would you—?'

She pressed a finger against his lip. 'Don't say it. Because we're not going to take anything for granted,' Amy said. 'Don't say a word to me until you've talked it over with Perdy—and I want you to make sure she knows that I love her but I'm not expecting her to pretend Eloise never existed. That'd be completely wrong. Her mum will always be her mum, and it's fine for Perdy to talk about her and look at her photographs—and we can both help her remember the good times and put the bad memories behind her.'

'So, hypothetically,' Tom said, 'if Perdy says yes and if you say yes, we'd be talking about a house somewhere in the village, with a garden for a slide, a swing and a trampoline.'

'And a puppy. Don't forget the puppy,' Amy added. 'Provided Perdy says yes for all of us. No counting chickens. If she says no, then it's a no.'

Tom smiled. 'And if she says yes?'

'Then I'll say yes, too.'

He kissed her, very gently. 'I have a good feeling about this...'

CHAPTER FOURTEEN

Six months later

CASSIE had insisted on tradition—especially as Amy and Tom were marrying in the tiny eleventh-century church in the centre of the village—so Perdy and Amy had spent the night before the wedding at Marsh End House rather than at their own house in the village.

On the Saturday morning, Perdy sat patiently while Beth finished painting her nails, and Alexis did the same as Cassie painted hers. Laura finished arranging the veil over Amy's hair, then stepped back to admire her best friend.

'What do you think?' she asked the others.

'Beautiful,' they chorused.

'You're a radiant bride, Amy,' Laura said with a smile.

'Thank you—and it looks as if I've got radiant brides-maids and matrons of honour, too,' Amy said.

'It helps that Sam's started sleeping through the night,' Beth said feelingly, 'or I would've needed so much con-cealer under my eyes, I'd have been charged excess baggage before I got on the plane.'

'Beth, you'd manage to look glamorous wearing a hessian sack,' Amy said, laughing.

'This is going to be such a cool wedding. I'm going to have a proper family,' Perdy said.

'Absolutely,' Amy agreed. True to Tom's prediction, Perdy had been delighted when Tom had asked her whether she'd like Amy to be a permanent part of her life, and Tom had called the jeweller's the second the shop had opened to order one very special engagement ring: an eternity symbol made from diamonds, flanked by Paraiba topaz. Amy and Perdy's birthstones.

'And we're getting BT next week.' BT—named by Perdy, and short for 'Buster Two'—was the chocolate Labrador puppy Tom had taken them to see three weeks before and which they'd all agreed would be the perfect addition to their family.

The last few months had been a whirl. To Amy's surprise, she hadn't been offered a locum post; she'd been offered her dream job, instead, setting up a treatment centre at the hospital forty minutes down the road. It was a similar commute to the one she'd had in London, and both Tom and Perdy had told her to take the job.

Joe, on his return to England, had said that he wanted to cut his hours down and offered Tom a full-time post at the practice—with the new housing development at the edge of the village, the practice had to expand and he thought Tom was perfect for the job.

And then there was moving into the house in the middle of the village, an old place that needed a little bit of work but which had a large garden and Perdy could see the sea from her bedroom window.

Not to mention wedding preparations. Amy's parents were even flying over from America for a couple of days—though, true to form, they were shoehorning it around their work and were arriving at the very last minute: they planned to meet everyone at the church then go back to America the following day. But Amy didn't mind because she had Cassie and Joe, and Tom's parents had proved to be as warm as Tom himself, accepting her immediately as part of their son's life. She'd written a letter to Eloise's parents, explaining that she wasn't taking Eloise's place and they'd always have a warm welcome if they wanted to visit Perdy, and Tom had been astonished when Eloise's mother had called to say thank you.

'So, let's run through the last checks. Flowers?' Laura asked.

'All here and looking fabulous,' Cassie said. 'Joe's taken the buttonholes and the rest of the corsages to the church—he'll be back any second now.' Joe had arranged to step into his brother's shoes and accompany Amy in the wedding car, and if the flight was delayed he'd be the one to give the bride away.

Beth looked at her watch. 'The car should be here in ten minutes and the photographer will be here any moment now. Bridesmaids all present and correct?' Beth asked.

'Yes,' Perdy and Alexis chorused.

'Matrons of honour?' Cassie asked.

'We're ready,' Beth said.

'And Ben's waiting for us at the church,' Laura said.

'I'm so pleased he's well enough to make it,' Amy said. 'His recovery has been amazing.'

'He's never going to walk again,' Laura said, 'but he can do most things.'

Amy noticed that Laura was fiddling with the neckline of her dress. 'Are you all right, Laura?' she asked.

'Mmm. Obviously I've been stuffing my face too much over the last week,' Laura said ruefully. 'I meant to be good, but I've been starving.'

Amy raised an eyebrow. 'Your dress is too tight at the top, and you're permanently hungry? Hmm. Right, you're on mineral water today. No more than one sip of champagne at the toast.'

'What?' Laura frowned.

'I second that,' Cassie said, 'as a GP's wife.'

'And I third it, as a GP's daughter,' Beth added. 'Not to mention that the same thing happened to me almost exactly a year ago so I know exactly what you mean. I ate like a horse.'

Laura stared at them all, clearly doing rapid mental calculations. 'Oh. My. God.'

'Would I be right in saying six weeks?' Beth asked, arching an eyebrow.

'I've been trying not to think about it and get my hopes up, just in case.' Laura dragged in a breath. 'It's too early to say anything. Not until twelve weeks and I'm really sure.'

'We won't say a word to anyone,' Amy promised. 'But you've just made today even more special.'

'Why?' Perdy asked.

'Grown-up stuff,' Amy said, giving her a hug. 'But I'll tell you why today's incredibly special: it's because I'm marrying you and your dad.'

'And it's special for me because I'm a bridesmaid and I'm getting a second mum,' Perdy said.

Amy had to swallow the lump in her throat, and hugged Perdy just that little bit tighter.

But the lump in her throat deepened when the next knock on the door turned out to be the florist again—this time with a red rose for herself and a pink one for Perdy. And both had the same message, in Tom's surprisingly neat handwriting: 'I love you. And I can't wait until we're officially a family.'

'Nobody's ever sent me flowers before,' Perdy said, beaming. 'I love Daddy—and I love you, Amy.'

'I love you, too.' Amy had to blink back the tears.

The photographer arrived and took a few 'getting ready' pictures; then the cars arrived.

'OK, love?' Joe asked, squeezing her hand.

She nodded. 'Thanks for agreeing to step into Dad's shoes. I don't think I could've faced this bit on my own.'

'I think of you as one of mine anyway,' Joe said, 'and I'm thrilled to bits that you asked me. I hope for your sake that your father's plane is on time, but if it isn't that's no reflection on you.'

'I know. You and Cassie have taught me that. You both kept me grounded and you always made me feel loved.'

'Because you are loved,' Joe said softly. 'You look fabulous. And I know you're going to be happy with Tom. He's a good man.'

'The best,' Amy agreed.

Tom, waiting at the altar, glanced at his watch.

Ben wheeled his chair up towards him. 'Relax,' he advised. 'They'll be here on time. Amy's never been late in all the years Laura's known her.'

'Mmm.' But there was always a first time.

Ben patted his hand. 'This is the worst bit. Waiting. But the moment you turn round and see her walking up the aisle to you—that's the best in the world. Knowing that the rest of your life is going to start here, and whatever fate throws at you you'll get through it because she's by your side.'

'That's true.' It hadn't been true of his marriage to Eloise, but Tom knew that Amy was different. She was just as ambitious and just as determined—but she made time for him and Perdy, just as he would always make time for her.

There was a flurry at the other end of the church, and Tom heard the music change to Pachelbel's Canon. He turned round to watch his bride walk down the aisle towards him on her father's arm, followed by his daughter and the other three bridesmaids, and his heart swelled in his chest; he loved Amy and Perdy so very much.

As Amy joined him at the aisle, she smiled at him through her veil.

'I love you,' he mouthed.

'I love you, too,' she mouthed back.

'We have come together in the presence of God, to witness the marriage of Amy and Tom, to ask his blessing on them, and to share in their joy,' the rector said solemnly.

And Tom knew that the joy would be everlasting.

* * * * *

MEDICAL™ 2-in-1

Ambition. Passion. Scandal.

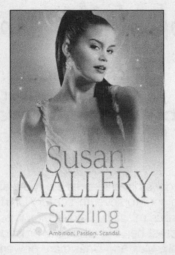

Cold, powerful matriarch Gloria controls the Buchanan dynasty. But, after falling ill, she's forced to rely on home help Lori Johnson.

Lori has struggled out of poverty and has no time for spoiled playboy Reid Buchanan. Especially when he's embroiled in a tabloid sex scandal.

Lori must show the Buchanans what's really important – before secrets and lies destroy them all.

Susan Mallery's Buchanan Dynasty –
secrets are about to be revealed…

Available 6th August 2010

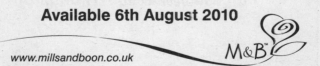

www.millsandboon.co.uk

2 FREE BOOKS
AND A SURPRISE GIFT

We would like to take this opportunity to thank you for reading this Mills & Boon® book by offering you the chance to take TWO more specially selected books from the Medical™ series absolutely FREE! We're also making this offer to introduce you to the benefits of the Mills & Boon® Book Club™—

- **FREE home delivery**
- **FREE gifts and competitions**
- **FREE monthly Newsletter**
- **Exclusive Mills & Boon Book Club offers**
- **Books available before they're in the shops**

Accepting these FREE books and gift places you under no obligation to buy, you may cancel at any time, even after receiving your free books. Simply complete your details below and return the entire page to the address below. You don't even need a stamp!

YES Please send me 2 free Medical books and a surprise gift. I understand that unless you hear from me, I will receive 5 superb new stories every month including two 2-in-1 books priced at £4.99 each and a single book priced at £3.19, postage and packing free. I am under no obligation to purchase any books and may cancel my subscription at any time. The free books and gift will be mine to keep in any case.

Ms/Mrs/Miss/Mr _____ Initials _____

Surname _____
Address _____

_____ Postcode _____
E-mail _____

Send this whole page to: Mills & Boon Book Club, Free Book Offer, FREEPOST NAT 10298, Richmond, TW9 1BR